Francis Silas Chata

Christian Truths

Lectures

Francis Silas Chatard

Christian Truths
Lectures

ISBN/EAN: 9783741187421

Manufactured in Europe, USA, Canada, Australia, Japa

Cover: Foto ©Andreas Hilbeck / pixelio.de

Manufactured and distributed by brebook publishing software
(www.brebook.com)

Francis Silas Chatard

Christian Truths

CHRISTIAN TRUTHS.

LECTURES

BY THE

RT. REV. FRANCIS SILAS CHATARD, D.D.,

BISHOP OF VINCENNES.

New York:

THE CATHOLIC PUBLICATION SOCIETY CO.,

9 BARCLAY STREET.

—

1881.

CONTENTS.

 Contents.

LECTURE VIII.

LECTURE IX.

LECTURE X.

LECTURE XI.

PREFACE.

O^F the Lectures published in this volume
the first four were given during the past
winter in St. John's Church, Indianapolis, and
from the interest they excited I am led to
hope they will not be without a beneficial influence. The remainder, with the exception of
the last, were delivered during my residence in
Rome. The citations they contain will be of
assistance to Catholic young men in strength-
ening their faith and supplying them with
means to defend it. The last lecture, on "Early Christianity," is, as is seen on reading it,
one of those matter-of-fact arguments which
are appreciated to-day more than ever, and it
cannot fail to have its weight. I am in duty
bound to give credit to the illustrious archæologist, Commendatore G. B. de Rossi, author
of the *Roma Sutterranea*, for nearly all the in-

formation I lay before the reader in this lecture, though I have frequently studied the frescoes and monuments I refer to on the spot.

My aim in publishing this book has been to
furnish our young Catholics with a manual
which will be useful to them in meeting the
vital questions of the day in a manner suited
to parry the attacks against the faith. The
only merit I may claim for it is that I have
striven to be very exact in all my quotations,
having, as far as memory serves me, verified
them all in the best editions before using them,
where that was possible. Certainly, no one
need feel himself in any danger of going
astray in trusting the citations.

In conclusion I submit, as becomes a bishop
of the Catholic Church, all I have here written
to the supreme and infallible authority of the
Head of the Church, the Vicar of Christ on
earth, ready to correct any error into which I
may have fallen; and I pray that God, who
alone "gives the increase," through the intercession of the ever-blessed and immaculate Virgin Mary, may illumine the mind and touch

the heart of those who read, that they may appreciate still more, and more ardently love, the faith, without which "it is impossible to please God." *

✠ FRANCIS SILAS CHATARD,
Bishop of Vincennes.

INDIANAPOLIS, IND., April 9, 1881.

* St. Paul, Heb. xi. 6.

LECTURE I.

THE PERSONALITY OF GOD.

ANY one who gives even a passing attention to current literature cannot but be aware of the widely-disseminated teachings that aim not only at the destruction of revelation, but even at the existence of God. No one who has the best interest of the human family at heart can fail to be exceedingly pained to witness the defection from the ranks of believers in revealed religion of so many of the young, energetic, and talented men of to-day. This painful fact—for fact it is—is a mystery to many and defies their efforts at explanation. But from the Catholic standpoint there is no mystery whatsoever in the matter. Catholic theology teaches that faith is a gift of God ; she takes the truth of this from the lips of her Divine Founder. She knows that

faith, being a gift, is not a part of man's nature
—not essential to it, that is, in a natural way,
as man's reason is essential to him—and that,
therefore, he can be without it, while his natural qualities and endowments remain the same.
She knows that this gift of faith, not being
essential, after having been once possessed can
be lost. With this knowledge, my dear friends,
we are prepared to see men without faith, and
to see men lose it also. And when we look
around and see the present state of the world
we are not surprised at the absence and loss of
faith, though pained at this beyond power of
expression; for to recognize the claims of faith
requires a spirit of prayer and of conscientious
investigation. Abroad we see a forgetfulness of
God, and a levity of manner in treating of spiritual matters, inimical to all serious reflection
and study. To preserve the faith once had is
requisite a spirit of humble submission to God,
coupled with a good moral life. A spirit of
pride, especially pride of intellect, whereby a
man worships himself and looks down on others,
and a life of sensuality, sap and destroy faith.
Now look around on the world as you know it,
and tell me whether pride and sensuality, in
giant form, are not stalking it over the land?

Therefore is it that we are not surprised at the loss or absence of faith among the masses.

But it is the duty of all those who are, by the providence of God, named to preside over their fellow-men as teachers of the Gospel to do all they can to remedy this state of things, to give the faith to those who have it not, and to lead back to the fold those who have lost it, by showing clearly the truth, its beauty and consistency, and how it may be acquired and retained. And for this reason, my dear friends, I take to-day the most fundamental of all truths, upon which all others depend—the existence of God Himself, the personality of God, that is; for a God who is not personal is no God at all.

To show this great and all-important truth in its proper light, I refer to the absolute requirement on the part of the human intellect of a cause. The intellect of man is the supreme judge in this matter. The mind we have is that whereby we recognize the truth. There is no other tribunal but the mind of man, anterior to his full recognition of God's claims on his submission. The Catholic Church does not unduly exalt the human intellect; she does not allow the mind of man to sit in judgment on what God has revealed, except in so far as it may reverently explain and apply it to the needs of our nature. But while she thus curbs it, she does not despise the power of human reason. On the contrary, she honors it, recognizes its capacity and aspirations, guards and defends it. The Catholic Church ever protects man's intellect from what might mar it by excess or by defect. As an instance of the way in which she saves it from going to extremes, I may mention the consistent, firm opposition she has ever made to the doctrine of private judgment, so vaunted by non-Catholics, and so little made use of by them. She has always maintained the doctrine that God speaks to man through His Church on earth ; and for this reason she denies that the Spirit of God is with each one to constitute him a judge of the meaning of the Sacred Text, the interpretation of which lies with the Holy Spirit residing in the Church and speaking through those of whom Christ said : "He who hears you, hears me." And in so deciding, it strikes me, she speaks in accord with the requirements of reason itself.

On the other hand, the Church has unmistakably asserted the powers of the mind of man, against those who sought unduly to disparage it. Of this I could cite you several instances. For example, there was a school of men that sprang from the religious movements of the sixteenth century, which held that man, in his present condition, is incapable of doing any good work pleasing to God, and that even all his actions are bad. The Catholic Church taught, on the contrary, that our actions depend for their morality on the way in which our conscience judges; so that an act of idolatry, for instance, which is a sin of great gravity if the one committing it knows he is doing wrong, comes to be no sin at all if a man is in good faith. This same school, or those akin to it, went so far as to deny the power of knowing anything above what we see about us, and required a tradition to initiate men into an elementary knowledge of the most important or obvious truths. The Catholic Church repelled such teaching, by proclaiming that man's mind has an innate power of arriving at truth by the faculties of observation, self-study, reasoning, and abstraction. Another school thought so little of any powers inherent in man as to require a vision of God Himself, a natural revelation, that he might know the primal truths, and went so far as to say man could not act on material things, but that, on or by occasion of them, God cooperated and did whatever was external to the thought. All these ideas have been more or less condemned or discountenanced by the Catholic Church, which teaches tho power of man's mind is so great, that, by the contemplation of what exists, he can attain to the knowledge, not only of truth, but of the existence of God and of His power and wisdom, though not so as to comprehend them fully.* With the approbation, therefore, of the Catholic Church on the native powers of the mind of man, let us see whither this mind leads us in our search after the personality of God.

If there is anything a man's mind is active about, it is in finding "the reason of a thing," the cause of it. No man practically believes in chance. It is never taken as an excuse for crime. The use of this word *chance* serves simply to cover an ignorance of what produced the fact we have to deal with. Nothing comes into being without *a cause*, and the human race has always accepted and has always held the doctrine of causality. The whole system of scientific enquiry is based on it; no science ever existed without taking it for granted. Pre-eminently does the inductive process, so much, and in great part, so justly lauded nowadays, start from the

* Vatican Council, Constitutio Dogmatica. ch. iv.

principle of causality, of cause and effect. The disciple of physical science observes with the greatest care all phenomena ; he classifies them and waits patiently. And why ? That he may, by comparing and carefully analyzing, discover the cause of the phenomena ; and this he will call the law or the simple cause. It is in this way the great discoveries have been made; in this way Galileo found out, or conjectured rather, the motion of the earth ; thus Newton discovered the law of gravity ; after this manner scientific men traced the cause of health or of disease—the diseases so well known that come from the use of bad food or from the introduction into the system of infusoria.

Here, then, we have the whole scientific world bent on the study of cause and effect. The verdict of the minds of men, our only criterion, is in favor, most pronouncedly, of cause, of causality.

Is it not illogical, my friends, to have such a habit of mind, and still to stop short at the last cause or first cause of all? There must be a first cause ; there is no escape from this. If you stop short at your last material cause, you must make it your first cause and put up with the absurd consequences. If it be your first cause it must have produced itself ; it must have life in itself ;

it must be self-existent; it must be infinite, unlimited, because nothing existed before it to limit
it, and it could not limit itself. It must be sim-
ple--not composed of elements, that is; not material, for composition implies one who composed
or formed the composite. It must be unchangeable, for change involves unrest; and a being infinitely perfect, possessing all in itself, cannot
change for the better, much less for the worse,
since this would argue imperfection; so that it
must have perfect rest in itself. Are you prepared to assert all this of matter as you know it
and see it? The pantheist says the first cause is
no higher than this world we see around us; this
world itself is God. Yet the pantheist believes
in primal imperfection, in change from good to
better; in evolution; in such a progress, that this
God of his becomes conscious of himself in man!
Was there ever a greater contradiction? He
cannot escape from the direct consequences I
have just laid before you, and yet he denies to
his God the attributes of intelligent consciousness until his God has developed into man!

Look at man and study him as he is. What
do you remark in him especially? Not only
his intellect and his energy; but you see one
quality pre-eminent: he has the absolute control

of his being; he rules it supreme. His mind
feeds upon whatsoever object he turns it to;
his will loves that which he has judged suit-
able for him; his freedom constitutes him a responsible being; his fellow-men hold him responsible for his acts. This is the noblest type
of existence with which we come in contact;
and this nobility of type is due to the fact
that man is a *person*. A man has personality—
the adequate principle, that is, of his actions;
for personality is that rational mode of existence which renders a being independent of others and the adequate principle of his actions,
so that his actions are his own. For this reason
is he responsible. This mode of existence can
be conceived of as capable of being separated
from human nature; so that we conceive of it as
something which gives perfection to human nature; though there may be a higher personality
given to human nature—as, for example, the personality of an angel; or, better still, as happened
in the mystery of the Incarnation, according to
the theology of the Church, the Personality of
the Son of God. Now, here is a quality of the
very highest order existing in man. Is it possible we are going to deny it in the first cause
of all things, which we saw a moment ago must

have been, from the very nature of things, possessed in the very beginning of every perfection?
There can be no effect without a cause ; how are
we to account for the existence of personality in
man, if it did not first exist in God? Then,
again, we conceive of God as the greatest and
most perfect of beings, and we cannot exclude
personality from God without degrading the very
idea of this Supreme Being and subjecting this
God thus degraded to a law of evolution He did
not make. And who made it for this God?
Fate? destiny? Then fate or destiny is God,
and we have the same trouble over again. It is
the fable of the ancients once more.

Again, let us look at man. We find him in
this age of ours engaged in all manner of material development, nowhere more so than in
this country we live in. Inventions of every
kind are daily presented to the Patent Office and
patents are secured. Now, I want to know on
what ground these patents are given? Here is
a wonderful piece of machinery—the cotton-gin
or threshing-machine. If this object, this cotton-
gin or threshing-machine, came by chance, developed out of matter by itself, what right has
the government to give a man a patent for it, to
allow him the exclusive privilege of making and

selling it? Manifestly there is no right in the question. No man, under such circumstances, has a right to a patent, and the government is wrong, unjust, oppressive to grant such privileges. But I can fancy the intelligent inventors of our country, who have made its name famous throughout the civilized world; I can fancy every man who has aspirations to invent something useful for his fellow-men and profitable to himself; I can fancy all these smiling a scornful smile at the unfortunate wight who would insinuate that their work was mere chance-work, nothing more; that their application of principles discovered was not their own brain-work. The whole world honors the inventor and gives him credit for what he has done for them; they even call him the benefactor of his kind, while they bow in homage at his power of mind. This is instinctive; and it is because the order, and adaptability, and results witnessed in his work convince all that it came from the mind of a man of genius, gifted with personality which ruled and rightly directed his faculties, and finally led to such happy results. A man who has lost his personality—or, what is nearly equivalent, the power to rule himself and act with judgment and order—could never do such things; and therefore are the order, and adaptability, and fitness of parts in his work an evidence of personality in man.

Raise your eyes from man and look to the First Cause of all things, and then consider His works. Behold the universe before you. See those countless stars, those worlds moving in space, revolving around their central orb, and that orb and its system, too, moving in order. Ask the mathematician and astronomer what they have observed. They will tell you that the sciences they cultivate are justly and preeminently known as " the exact sciences "; that all these movements they have for ages been watching are so regular that they can calculate to a second the place where a given planet will be ten or a hundred years hence. Do they not tell us with the utmost precision the eclipses of the sun and of the moon? Does not the United States Signal Service, one of the glories of our country, with a sureness almost unerring, warn us of what is to come upon us in the way of inclement weather? Have not numberless lives been saved this year by its timely warnings? What does all this prove but the most perfect order in nature? And man himself, with his intellect, and will, and wonderful mechanism of body,—is he not a perfect type of order in nature? And now, if you are so inclined to look with pitying contempt on the one who would rob an inventor of his glory and refuse him approbation as a man of genius, personality, and order, are you going to deny personality, the adequate principle of His acts, to the First Cause, from whom this universe came; from whose mind the laws of order and proportion we witness among the planets proceeded; whose hand fashioned this frame of ours and gave it the noble mind that makes man the lord of creation? It is absurd to think it, my friends; and you know this is your judgment, too.

A further point in this system of pantheism which denies God's personality is, that its results conflict with the unanimous judgment of past generations, and with that of the generation of this day in which we live. According to the pantheist, the only God there is is nature, and that God becomes conscious of Himself in the intellect of man, the most perfect endowment of the visible world. In other words, man is God. That is the formula. What is the result? If I am God, then I am a law to myself; there is no one to whom I must give an account. I can do as I please. I can do no wrong, for we can conceive of no wrong when there exists no law before us to which we can refer as the criterion of our actions. My will is the law, because I am God and there is nothing superior to me. What follows? Why, I can do as I please; and, provided I do not find some one who will not let me do as I please, I have no restraint on my actions. All idea of moral law, of responsibility is lost; all laws are without any other foundation but force and might. Is this the idea of civilized society? Is this the idea of pagan society? Is this the idea of even the savage? It is not. All men believe in right and wrong naturally. It is reserved for this our day to see and hear the contrary avowed and practised; and the result is licentiousness, disregard of vested rights and ownership of property, theft, communism, murder! Once destroy the idea of a personal God independent of and separate from matter, and such is the consequence—the absolute destruction of morality and the impossibility of social life.

To these most weighty reasons, which compel our mind to acknowledge the existence of a personal God, I may add the testimony of the

human race itself. In all ages, in every clime,
wherever man has been, there has man's soul
recognized the power of God and looked up
to Him as a Supreme Being, distinct from and
ruling the universe. The greatest and most
famed intellects, equally with the untutored
mind, have borne witness to this truth. We
turn over the pages of the great philosopher
Plato, and we read what he tells us of his
great master, the sage of Athens. In his work
known as *Timæus* * he introduces Socrates as
present with his disciples, and the discussion,
which goes on there, regards the existence of a
First Cause and the production, calling into
existence of all that is visible. A late writer
(Paul Janet) sums up the teaching of Socrates in these words: "Socrates does not only
see in nature the traces of intelligence, he recognizes the proofs of a power essentially good
and full of solicitude for men ; he believes in
the constant presence and infallible action of
this power in the whole universe. Socrates, in
fine, announced to the world the sublime dogma of Providence." † Plato—known as the

---

* Ed. Firmin-Didot, Paris, 1862.

† *Dictionnaire des Sciences Philosophique*, Frank, 1875, art. "Socrates,"
p. 1635, quoted by Abbé Alexis Arduin, *Cosmogonie.*

Divine Plato, from the near approach of his ideas about God to the teachings of revelation—in the work I have just referred to, the *Timæus*, expounds his views in unmistakable terms. He teaches that everything that is made, or has an origin, must of necessity proceed from a cause; for nothing can have an origin without a cause. He says the cause of all things is eternal. And he furthermore says: "We say of him that he was, is, and shall be, while the only thing proper to say of him is, that he *is*"; * in this way excluding succession or change in God, making Him eternal, immutable. As we hear this pagan philosopher thus instructing his disciples, we recall instinctively the name God gives Himself in the inspired text, "I am who am." In another place he exclaims: "In the name of God shall we be easily persuaded to believe the one, who *is* absolutely, has no movement, no life, no soul, no thought; that he is inert, that he has no august and holy intelligence? Shall we say he has intelligence but no life? Shall we say he has both the one and the other, but no personality? Shall we say he

---

*Ibi., p. 209, 25.

is personal, intelligent, living, but inert? All
this would be absurd!*

Another great philosopher of antiquity, Aristotle, in some respects perhaps greater than
Plato, though inferior to him in others, speaks
of God as the cause of all things: "For God,"
he writes in his first book of *Metaphysics*,† "is
seen to be the cause and certain beginning of
all things." He speaks of God as eternally
enjoying perfect happiness; and says that "in
Him there is life, for the action of the intelligence is life, and God is actual intelligence
itself; this intelligence, taken in itself, is His
perfect and eternal life."

I close with one more witness, one whose name
as a philosopher and orator has filled the world
for nigh two thousand years, and whose name will
be re-echoed in future generations when the gifted but superficial orators of to-day, whose voice
is raised against God, shall have been forgotten.
When those whose names are great before the
public in this day of ours will have sunk into
their graves, pitied by men for their folly in at-
tempting to destroy the belief of human nature
in God; and the oblivion of death, like a pall,

* Translation of F. Gratry.
† Book I. ch. ii., ed. P. de la Rovière, Aureliæ Allobrogum, an. 1605.

shall have settled upon them and for ever hid
them from the notice of men, the name of Mar-
cus Tullius Cicero will be hailed with pleasure,
his works will be read with profit and delight,
and for nothing will he be more honored than
for this; because he proclaimed absolutely the
existence of God. I cite but a few words from
among his eloquent writings on this subject:
"Whoever doubts that there is a God present
to us and all-powerful, I cannot understand
why he does not doubt about the existence of
the sun" (*De Nat. Deorum*, lib. ii. 2).* "It is
well known among all, by the judgment of all
peoples, that there are gods; what kind of
gods they are, is disputed; that they exist, no
one denies" (No. 5, ibi.) And he moreover
quotes Xenophon telling of Socrates asking,
"whence did man get this mind of his" except
from God, the first cause of all? (No. 6, ibi.)

In the second century of the Church there
lived a most learned man, full of talent and
fiery energy. He was a Christian and an able
asserter of the truths of his faith. This man
was the great Tertullian, the apologist, so-called, of Christianity. His pen was ever ready,
and he never shrank from a contest with the

---

* Ed. Jo. Ernesti, Londini, 1830, cur. A. J. Valpy.

false ideas of his day. He calls to his aid, in asserting the existence of the one true God, the soul of man. As he expressly states, he does not want the testimony of the soul of a man learned and experienced in the ways of the world; for, he says, no one now trusts learning, however slight it be. "I call up-on thee as a witness," he exclaims, address-ing the soul, "simple, rude, unpolished, un-tutored as thou art in those who have naught but thee; that very soul who art to be found wholly at the crossing, in the byway or humble workshop." What does such a soul say? It calls on God by naming Him constantly as sim-ply God, and exclaims: "God is good; God has done us good"; "God sees." "O testimony!" he cries out—"O testimony of a soul naturally Christian! And when it says this it does not look toward the Capitol, but up to heaven, for it knows the dwelling-place of the living God." Such has always been the testimony of the soul to the existence of God. It cannot help itself, for God made nature; nature is the teacher, and the soul the disciple.* It is no wonder, then, my dear friends, that Christianity triumphed over paganism. No wonder that we have eloquent

* Tertullian, *De Testimonio Animæ.*

monuments of that victory. Let me trespass for a moment longer on your time, that I may speak of but one. There is a church in the city of Rome known as the Church of St. Clement, because the house of the Clement family, of which came St. Clement, pope and martyr, was converted into a church. In process of time the church having fallen into decay and being too low, the present church was built upon the foundations and walls, the under portion having been filled up with earth. I was in that city when the subterranean portions were dug out, and saw with my own eyes what was discovered. Among many other objects of great interest was found, beneath the magnificent and splendidly ornamented church above, a small, cave-like temple. Upon entering it, it was recognized to be a temple of Mithras, the god that represented heat—the heat of the sun especially—the god of fire, whose worship came from the East ; having been brought to Rome by Pompey the Great, the rival of Julius Cæsar. That worship flourished in Rome ; it burrowed beneath the temple of the great Capitoline Jove. It was the type of myths, and teemed with myths itself, and was pre-eminently pantheistic. What had happened to this god Mithras, here in the centre of the Ro-

man world, where he had chosen unto himself a
permanent abode? He was shut in by a Christian church; and there, on the floor of this his
temple, like Dagon of old, he lay with his neck
broken! Above him rose the majestic temple
of Christianity, whence daily go up, in this our
day, the prayers of the true worshippers of
God. Behold Christianity serenely triumphant
over paganism and pantheism!

I sum up briefly, my friends. God exists; He
is a pure spirit, infinitely perfect. He is distinct
from the world, endowed pre-eminently with personality more perfect than our own. He is the
first cause of all things. To Him we owe our being; to Him we owe our homage—the homage of
a good life. Even the pagan acknowledged this.
And I cannot close these remarks better than by
citing the words of the great Plato on this subject of a good life, in his letter to the relatives
and friends of Dion of Syracuse.* "God," he
says, "is a law to the wise, pleasure to the foolish." † Let us learn of this pagan; and if
there be any one here who has been led to fol-

---

* Plato, viii. Ep. ad Dionis., Proquinquos et Amicos, 34.
† Θεὸς δὲ ἀνθρώποις σώφροσι νόμος· αφροσι δὲ ἡδονή.

low the teachings of a false philosophy, let him pay homage to the united intellect of the world, and profess his belief in one true God and live according to His law.

LECTURE II.

---

*THE EXISTENCE OF THE SOUL IN MAN, ITS SIM-
PLICITY AND SPIRITUALITY.*

HAVING shown in my last lecture that God is, that He is a spirit infinitely intelligent, self-existent, and the Author of all things, it becomes my duty now, my dear friends, to vindicate a second essential truth at the very foundation of Christianity, the existence of the Soul of man, its simplicity and its spirituality. One of the fruits of so-called progress in these days of ours is the absolute denial of the existence of anything not material, and therefore of the soul of man ; while another result is to make the intelligent principle in man a part of the divinity, to say, that the god of nature manifests himself in man, who is therefore god, inasmuch as the spiritual element in man is nothing but the god of the pantheist becoming conscious of himself and of his excellence and attributes. Against these two erroneous views of the nature of man it is my purpose to demonstrate that there is in man a principle, an essence, which we call the soul; which is created by God for union with the body of man; and which is not material or composed of elements, but is one, simple, and spiritual in its being, endowed with intellect and freedom of will, and therefore the responsible agent in man's acts.

Having spoken at length last Sunday of pantheistic error, I will not stop to speak further on this phase of it than to say, that such an idea is completely at variance with the thought and practical judgment of the human race. What are the results of this pantheistic teaching, man is God? Is it not that man has no superior; that there is therefore no law to bind him; that he is master of his actions in such a way as to be capable of doing no wrong; that all distinction of right or wrong is done away with? Yet what do men think about this matter? They believe in a law. They believe man is amenable to it, subject to it. They believe that there does exist a distinction between right and wrong; that the source of this distinction is in the eternal fitness of things as God sees them.

They are profoundly convinced of man's responsibility for his acts. They are most intimately persuaded of his being a free agent. For this reason men make laws, enact penalties, and inflict these penalties on the transgressors of their laws. Were the supposition of the pantheist true, we should have the absurd spectacle of the god of pantheism punishing himself for what he does, without rhyme or reason; for if the soul is god its will is the only law; and because in one man this god does his own will, inasmuch as he exists in other men, he chastises himself. So absurd a consequence could not but result from such a monstrous error as pantheism. The intellect and the moral sense of man alike scout the idea that there is a portion of the Deity in man, that man is God. Reason is our tribunal; and reason decides.

There is more difficulty in answering the materialist, however, than in showing the contradictions of pantheism. And yet the difficulty is not so great that materialism cannot, with a little effort of attention and reasoning, be easily shown inconsistent with all reason teaches us, and therefore unworthy of the acceptance of a rational being.

The cardinal principle of the materialist is that there is nothing but matter. Under the head of materialists are to be classed the positivists, evolutionists who evolve everything out of matter, and those who profess a belief in the indefinite progress, in a material sense, of nature. For all these theories are based on the development of matter. To these are to be added a horde of scientific men who, without any special preconceived ideas, from their observation of the laws of matter in the more perfect animal organisms, of involuntary muscular action, of reflex action in man and in the animals, of the movement of matter—of a limb, even after severance from the parent trunk, have leaped to the conclusion that thought is but a secretion of the brain, and that there is no such thing as a soul. It is useless to deny the gravity of this error, its great danger, its most destructive consequences. For this reason I have taken it as the subject of my second lecture, proposing to show the impossibility of matter thinking, and the absolute necessity, and therefore the existence, of a spiritual essence in man, thinking and ruling his acts, which is his soul, the principle of his actions, and the responsible agent of them.

By matter is understood by all that which is composed of elements, of parts, and can be divided; which has extension and occupies space. It is, moreover, inert; that is, does not move itself; and when it does move, it moves in consequence of a motor or moving power, and then it moves necessarily in the direction of the force or power that acts upon it.   I invite your attention particularly to these qualities of matter, its extension, form, and shape, its inability to move itself, and its necessary movement in the direction of the force that acts upon it; for I shall make special use of these facts in a moment.

If we turn our eyes upon ourselves, as it were inwardly, and consider what we are conscious of as going on within us, we have at once an idea of our identity; that is, we are conscious we are the same person we were always.   Changes have gone on around us; this body of ours even has changed; but there is a something in us that has not changed: it is that which did years ago what we are sorry for now, or what we are glad we did.   Again, that something which is in us rules our action.   It resolves, it acts with deliberation and promptness, it makes every part of the body act, all parts together, for one purpose—for example, for self-pre-

servation—with incredible rapidity. It is like
the engineer who is driving his engine, or a
man who is managing a pair of spirited horses;
his action makes all go together and work
without interfering the one with the other.
We are conscious there is a something in
us which acts in this way, and feel there
is no discussion or agreement between several
principles of being in us to produce so harmonious a result. The very quickness with which
we get out of danger precludes discussion,
deliberation, agreement. To deliberate would
mean destruction. There is, therefore, no multitude of counsellors, but one directing power.
Now, this can be only on the supposition that
this something is simple, not composed of
parts; the very complex nature of man's body
exacts this. To consist of parts would imply
the necessity of these different parts consulting, advising, agreeing, or refusing to agree,
if they were capable of doing this. Therefore
is it that this principle in us which is one,
identically one; which is one in its direction of
the forces of body; one in all its operations
whether of mind or of body—of thought, that
is, or of physical action—must be one by nature, not compound, not consisting of parts

added to parts, and therefore simple in its essence or being—simple, and not compound, not a composite. For the acts of any being are in accordance with its nature; while its nature can be judged of from its acts. Besides, we are conscious that we move ourselves. We say now and then we are moved to do something; but we mean that. considerations of various kinds have influenced our thoughts so as to make us resolve to do it. All the time we are conscious we move ourselves; that we needn't unless we wish; that we can do just the opposite, if we desire. Reason tells us this is a quality matter has not; and this being the case, what has that quality isn't matter, isn't this inert mass that can't move unless something moves it. Just contrast the work of this principle of action in us with that remarkable phenomenon called "reflex action." In ourselves we may see both. A blow to a nerve will cause immediate and spasmodic action of a limb which apparently has no connection with the nerve. But this is the result of mechanical action, irritating a nerve and thus stimulating the nervous system, and is determined to one thing or act, and we are conscious that this act goes on independently *of us;* that is, I am conscious this movement in me takes place without any control or direction of the thinking principle in me; whereas when I am self-possessed and direct my actions, such actions are mine, not those of my nerves or of my body. Is not this the way all men talk, and is it not the judgment of our tribunal—reason? Therefore we are always, in a natural, easy way, distinguishing between the action of matter and the action of the one, simple, self-ruling, self-directing principle in us; and this could not be, unless we were intimately persuaded that we had something in us not of matter, but of an order above matter and better than it, differing from it essentially in its nature.

One—the greatest—faculty of this principle in us, which we call the soul, is thought. This is its life, in fact. This belongs as essentially to the soul as breath does to the body. Now, with reference to thought, we are conscious that there is a unity in thought which does not admit of division. We recognize successive steps or stages in thought; but each thought is one in itself. It may be more or less distinct, yet it is always one. Men speak of half a mind; but this is a metaphorical ex-

pression signifying that they are not fully resolved. To speak of thought as having form,
shape, color, would cause people to look at
you with undisguised astonishment, possibly
with disagreeable surmises. To us all thought
is as fully present, as indivisible, as is the
simplicity of the soul itself; and it cannot
be otherwise; for, as I have said, thought is
the life of the soul, and if the one excludes
division the other must, too. Thought, therefore, cannot be conceived of as having extension, form, shape, color. What results from
this? That the soul is simple, not composed
of matter; for if it were, the thoughts would
be according to its nature and consist of
parts, and consequently there would be nothing strange in speaking of a half, or of a
quarter of a thought.

Again, thought cannot result from motion of
particles of matter. The reason of it is this:
matter is inert and moves only in consequence
of force applied to it; moreover, as I have already said, it moves necessarily in the direction of the force acting on it. Here, then, is an
additional reason which convinces us of the simplicity of the soul, for we are conscious of the
freedom of our thoughts. We can interrupt

them at will; we can, by the interior force of our volition, pursue an entirely different train of thought. We can check our mind so as to not let it reach a conclusion; or, having reached a conclusion, not permit our will to carry out the result. This freedom of thought is absolutely in contradiction to that necessary or compulsory movement such as belongs to matter. Besides, the necessity also of moving in the direction of the force impelling takes away all responsibility; for free-will is destroyed. Man is no longer a free agent; he becomes material wholly, and acts are organic changes in matter for which he is not answerable. These acts are not his; for the movement which produces such changes is from outside, and the changes are absolutely determined in extent and direction by the outside force. Here the materialist finds himself at once in conflict with the firm persuasion and belief of human reason from the beginning; for men have always recognized the responsibility of man with regard to his actions, and have made laws on that account. The very existence of all law presupposes, as a necessary condition, the freedom of man's will, his power to rule himself, the full possession of his faculties of action—his personality, in fine. Reason, therefore, is with us in asserting unmistakably the existence of the soul of man as a simple substance, with a life of thought and reason and of freedom of action which constitute it a spiritual being—a spirit.

Moreover, the materialist, whatever his theory, is often embarrassed for language, as he cannot find expressions which are not more or less, as Mr. Mallock has so fitly remarked, in accord with the teaching that man is a spirit; the reason of this is that words are the representations of man's ideas; and man has not the words which would please the materialist, because he has not such ideas—the ideas correspond to such words. Nothing daunted by this, however, the materialist professes his belief in evolution, and asserts that new desires produce new attempts of nature, and consequently new results. Now, here is a most illogical statement. Call to mind what I said a moment ago. If there is nothing but matter this matter moves necessarily according to the force impinging on it, and also necessarily in the direction of the same force. Not only this, which would, as you see, give all the credit of development to a power above matter and moving it; but as a stream rises no higher than its source, as you cannot make gold out of iron, or silk out of cotton, so you cannot get ideas above matter out of matter; you cannot produce thought from matter; you cannot have desires, manifesting themselves as a result of movement of matter, which are above matter itself. And for this reason the assertion that evolution is a result of material action only, having aspirations above itself, is not only untenable but absurd. That there are aspirations in beings endowed with reason and intellect is due to the fact that they have a soul at once simple and spiritual. In beings of a lower order which have no reason nor intellect, but only a soul simple in its substance, there can be no such aspirations, as those souls are bound down to a material life, and are not intended, and are not able to rise above that material level.

But by far the—I will not say strongest, but—most impressive argument to make us appreciate the spiritual nature of the soul is the practical one whereby men judge of the worth of anything. What are its natural results? The tree is known by its fruits. What are the fruits of materialism? At one stroke it blots out the very thought and idea of everything spiritual, everything exalting, everything, I may say, sublime. There is nothing left but the brute, dread force of nature. A frightful precipice or a fearful crash of thunder will inspire fear, but not raise the mind higher than the yawning gulf or the affrighting sound of nature's workings. The simple Indian who walked amid the forests of this land of ours here, was wrong to think of the Great Spirit when the fierce winds raged over the earth, tore up giant oaks by the roots; when the blinding flash gleamed across the lowering, dark vault of heaven, and the thunder spoke of irresistible power! He was a savage; he knew no better; he had not reached the culture and elevated plane of thought of the man of science in the nineteenth century! He was wrong to think of anything but matter; for, as the materialist says, nothing but matter exists.

Closely following on this result or fruit comes another—the destruction of all morality. This is a necessary consequence of the system of materialism, and it is openly avowed by its followers. If any still hold back in this avowal it is because they do not appreciate where they stand and are not well up in their tenets. This is evident; because no morality or moral law can be conceived of unless we have a lawgiver. Laws are not framed with reference to the one who makes them, but to bind and direct others. In the supposition that there is no moral lawgiver there can be no moral law; and not only no moral law as laid down by revelation, but no natural moral law, no system of ethics, no rights and no duties, rights and duties springing from the natural law. Therefore the only controlling principle, according to materialism, is might. Might makes right; that is the formula, the outcome of materialism. Again all duty of self-control vanishes; passion, the gratification of all desires, provided it can be done so as not to interfere with material well-being, is to be allowed full sway. There is no check upon it. Why, last summer a professor addressing a class of young men in Paris, on occasion of their graduation, bade them remember that virtue was but a name; that such an idea was but a trammel; that talent only was the thing to look to in a man who was to rise and hold position and authority, and ended by saying: "Henceforth, gentlemen, pleasure is to be your measure of action." What wonder that we see the consequences of such teaching in that unfortunate country and elsewhere amid the votaries of materialism? Communism is the necessary result of materialism and positivism. The will of the masses is fast becoming the only criterion of what is right or wrong. It would be the law of the future, did materialism triumph; and murder, and arson, and crime in general would be good works, provided the masses willed them. Do we not see indications of this already? Defiance to what has hitherto been deemed law, and virtue, and morality is openly manifested, the outcome of this modern civilization, which has its foundation and its whole being in matter. Parents who are solicitous for the virtue and well-being of their children cannot, unless blunted by passion themselves, look on such a state of things without concern; and the feeling they have is the best condemnation of the system of materialism which, denying the existence of God, of the human soul, and of the hereafter, destroys every influence that can hold in check the depraved yearnings of the human heart.

Such is the testimony of the human soul; we are therefore prepared to have a like testimony from the human race. The human race has always believed in the existence of the soul, and in its being a free, responsible agent. This testimony is concordant. It has been given always, everywhere, and by all. I say all; for the small number hitherto rejecting belief in the existence of the soul is not to be considered. The fact shows this belief to be the true one, as we can gather from the well-known saying of Cicero : "Opinionum commenta delet dies ; veritatem confirmat" (*De Nat. Deorum*, ii.) —Time destroys the comments of opinion, but confirms the truth. For the universal judgment of men, always, everywhere the same, is the voice of nature ; and nature, as we saw last Sunday, in the words of Tertullian, is taught of God.

That the human race believed always in the existence of a spiritual element in man, which they called the soul, is evident to any one who is even a superficial student of history. The very fact that man worshipped God implies this. The belief in future rewards and punishments shows it. We can readily understand that if there is nothing but matter in the universe, nothing remains after a body is resolved into its material elements by death. This is the cardinal principle of materialism. Had men

believed this, every system of religion, of belief in rewards and punishments after death,
of morality, would have been an absurdity
on their part. But with all the force of their
mind the people clung to religious belief; they
avoided evil, that they might escape the punishment which, alike in India, in Greece, and at
Rome, were threatened after death to those who
transgressed the laws of nature or of religion.
The mythological systems of these countries,
known to every reader, even of an encyclopæ-
dia, tell of happiness with the gods as the consequence of a good life, as well as of the sufferings to be undergone by those who led a life
of crime. Such is the testimony of the human
race ; and this testimony is the testimony of
simple, unalloyed nature not debased by that
spirit of pride which eliminated God from the
universe. Granted that such belief and testimony are blurred and marred by innumerable
errors. That does not affect the main question,
the substance of the belief; they are but like
to the varied garb in which man arrays his
form, different according to climate or nation-
ality ; the form remains always the same—the
noble form of man. Just so this intimate persuasion of the human race in the existence of a

soul and in its future reward or future punishment, though attired in a garb which does not become it.

I willingly grant, as true, that among the cultured classes of all nations were to be found schools which were not in accord with this belief. The pantheism of the present day is not new. It is but a reproduction of that of Rome, of Greece, and of India. And the materialism of to-day had its progenitors not only in the disciples of Epicurus, but in the Buddhists of India and of China. Still the class of materialists was always a small one. The soul of man, unless immersed in pleasure, naturally revolts from holding such a tenet; and as a result the more intellectual took up a pantheistic system which identified the soul with God Himself.* The pantheists of all time taught the existence of a spirit in man distinct from the matter which formed his body, and therefore they ever rejected this monstrous theory which makes man naught save matter. But even among the heathen were to be found those who, rejecting these opposing errors as far as they knew them,

---

* Bauddhas of India and Fichte are identical in holding the exclusive existence of the τὸ ἐγώ. Brauchereau, *Hist. de la Philosophie*, p. 29, cites the *Précis de Quilly.*

taught the existence of the soul as we hold it, as a substance differing essentially from matter and made by God. Of all the great lights of antiquity the judgment of mankind has named as the greatest, Socrates, Plato, and Aristotle. The testimony of these three great men is enough to show us to what real culture and intellectual elevation can lead man. As a matter of fact, whatever the human mind of itself can produce is necessarily inferior to what can be known if the Maker of man unveils His treasure of knowledge. Still, the words of these men are admirable and most weighty. Xenophon, in his *Memorabilia*, tells us of Socrates deriving the existence of the soul from God. He is not only persuaded of its existence, but he absolutely excludes the possibility of the soul proceeding from matter, and of matter thinking. "Whence," he asks, "has man had this soul" except from God? Plato makes him speak, in his book entitled *Phædo*, of the immortality of the soul.*

Plato himself not only teaches the spiritual nature of the soul, but also a system of rewards and punishments to be undergone after

* § 68, Cary's translation.

death. He thus not only tells of the distinction between the soul and matter; he teaches, besides, that the soul can exist independently of matter.

Aristotle, so far from accepting materialistic ideas, believed so firmly in the existence of the soul that he wrote a book on its existence and qualities. In the beginning of this work he writes: "The soul is, as it were, the principle of all animals" (*De Anima*, l. i. c. i.) He goes on to tell us what those who preceded him thought, and then sums up as follows: "All define the soul by these three: motion, feeling, simplicity or absence of matter" (C. i. D. n. 486). He bears witness here to what has been the opinion of others who excluded matter from the soul. He does not accept, however, this definition, and lays down his own, styling the soul that which gives life to a human body capable of living; that which makes a body actually a living body: "Primus actus corporis potentiam vitæ habentis." * And so correct and proper has this definition been deemed that the Church, in her teaching on the

* Ἀναγκαῖον ἄρα τὴν ψυχὴν οὐσίαν εἶναι, ὡς εἶδος σώματος φυσικοῦ δυνάμει ζωὴν ἔχοντος. C. i. p. 480, D, ed. De la Rovière, 1605.

subject of the soul, has adopted it nearly in the same words : the soul is the form of the body—that is, according to the language of the schools, the soul is that which makes a human body a living body. He says, moreover, that the soul is a substance, and expressly argues against those who teach that it is composed of very subtle matter. He goes on to say that the soul must be comprehended, determined in its nature by its works ; and he treats of the various faculties of the soul—the senses, imagination and intellect.

It is evident from these citations, my dear friends, that the judgment of the humblest agrees with that of the most celebrated and brilliant of men in asserting the existence of the soul and its destiny. But striking and sublime as are their sentiments and ideas, these are little when we come to consider the way in which the Catholic Church speaks and decides with respect to the nature, and attributes, and future destiny of the soul. The theme is so grand it overwhelms one ; words fail. The greatest light of the Church, at this moment the patron of its theology, the great St. Thomas Aquinas, will tell us what is Catholic teaching on this subject. He was

a loving disciple of Aristotle and often uses
his language. After speaking of the existence
of the soul, which he declares incorporeal, and,
using the wording of Aristotle, calls the act
of the body, or that which makes a body actually a human body—the form of the body,
or that which makes a body a living body; he
goes on to specify that it is a spiritual essence, living and endowed with personality,
inasmuch as it is one with the body and the
adequate principle of life and action in man;
that it is only less than angelic in nature; that
it cannot see corruption; that its life is especially intellectual; that its destiny is to possess the Sovereign Truth and Sovereign Good.
St. Thomas Aquinas wrote with all the treasure of ancient knowledge at his command,
with the advantage of all the wonderful light
that came from the works of the great St. Augustine, whom he often quotes, and his mind
and his heart re-echoed the words of that great
African doctor: "Thou hast made us, O Lord!
for Thyself, and our heart is restless till it
find quiet in Thee!" There is the sublime
destiny of the human soul! Is it at all wonderful, my dear friends, that Christianity,
with such words on her lips, won the human

mind and gained the human heart? She came finding a civilization in a very high sense, cultured in the extreme, but with only a glimmer of light to raise man above himself and to free him from the thraldom of his passions. At once she made him see his condition, made him raise his eyes and look to his Father in heaven. She taught the inestimable value of a human soul; she made the great ones of the world, their princes and their rulers, recognize in the poor man a god-like nature—a nature God had made free with a freedom which God Himself respects. Her teachings made slavery in Europe a thing of the past, and her action, consistent with her teachings, raised the poor man from poverty and obscurity to the grand, pre-eminent position of ruler of the Church of God on earth. It was her doctrine on the rights of man which, triumphing over barbarism, heathen pride, and oppression of the lower classes, made the rights of man the basis of legislation, and consequently brought about the civilization of this period in which we live. Over those rights she has ever spread her ægis, and she will continue to do so, calumniated, though she has been and is, as the enemy of human liberty.

That liberty she asserts always and has ever asserted. She teaches that a man must act according to the dictates of his conscience, which is the voice of his soul; that everything done in accord with this voice is good, everything done against conscience is bad. She teaches that by faithful following of conscience only can a man reach his destiny. That destiny she makes us understand, by presenting us the spectacle of God Himself so valuing a human soul as to come after it, take human form, and die for it. Can anything so impress us with the idea of the excellence of the spiritual nature and supernatural destiny of a soul as this spectacle? Wonderful love and condescension of God! This sight, the God of heaven taking on Himself human nature, made the subduer of Attila, the great Pope Leo, transported with reverent admiration, burst forth in these words: "Recognize, O man! thy dignity, and, having been made a companion of the divine nature, return no longer by degenerate life to thy former vileness." Let us, with this great Doctor and benefactor of mankind, recognize the excellence and the dignity of our nature, of this soul of ours, and strive, by making

God its law, to save it from the thraldom of pleasure, and so prepare it for its destiny, the possession of Infinite Truth and Infinite Good —God Himself.

Lecture III.

IN the preceding two lectures, my dear friends, I have treated of the existence of God and of the existence of the human soul, of God and of His creature. It is evident that this creature, man, must be subject to his Creator. The very intellect he has, the reason he is endowed with, serve to make him know and regard with reverent awe the Supreme Being. He easily comes thereby to know his duty of adoration and of obedience. He has in his breast a still, small voice, which admonishes him of his duty neglected, or praises him for what he has well done. In the very fitness of things, as he sees and understands them, he finds a law of action regulating him. Led by these natural means, and much more by the traditions of the human race, he introduced various forms of honor to the Deity; varying religions came into existence; each people had its own peculiar form.

But it is one of man's frailties, that he is prone to err. He is fallible especially in regard to what excites his imagination and powerfully affects his feelings; and from this source of error sprang innumerable and discordant systems of belief and worship. Men deified everything that impressed them. It would be ludicrous, were it not so sad a spectacle, to call up in array the gods of paganism. Wise men felt this. Many rejected false worship in secret, and strove to offer to God some purer form of homage. But even here, so many were the ways of going astray, so often did men find it impossible to agree, that divisions without number occurred. In this state of the human mind men looked to heaven. They yearned for some safe guide. Plato, the great Plato, in the Dialogue in which Socrates takes part, makes Simmias avow man's inability to attain to certainty in belief unless he should have some divine word to teach him.* The sentiments of this philosopher but re-echoed that of the gene-

* *Phædo.*

rality of the human race. Man always yearned for union with Him from whom he came,
with God; he was ready to use any means
to effect it, and eagerly seized on any system
which promised to give him the light and
knowledge and moral power he sought. It
was this feeling cunning rulers availed themselves of to introduce their religious systems;
and to more effectually succeed, they feigned
intercourse with beings above nature. From
the founders of Hindu religions, from Brahma
and Buddha, to Numa and Mahomet, all
false systems of religious worship sought
their chief reliance in pretended supernatural
illumination; and this is one of the most ordinary accusations made against religious systems by rationalists, who do not believe in the
supernatural. The fact, however, that men do
look for something supernatural, for a communication from above, proves the deep-seat-
ed conviction of the human soul, that there
ought to be such a foundation for religious
worship; that it should come from God Himself. This is the persuasion of the mind of
man, expressed always and everywhere; this
the language of the soul. It is intimately persuaded that it is the child of God; that God,

as a father, should come to the aid of His children, enlighten their darkness, and let them know how they are to please Him. God is, in fact, the father of all. Fatherhood comes from Him, for its most perfect essence—fatherhood itself, that is—is in Him. Why is it that men condemn a father who turns his back on his offspring and abandons him to die? In the philosophy of those who argue in favor of improving the human race as one would stock, deformity or weakness would justify this. But such is not the language of the human race, for men characterize as *inhuman* such conduct. Whence comes this feeling, if not from the natural belief of man that a father must of necessity love his child, and provide for its welfare, in proportion to its inability to provide for itself? This is man's idea of fatherhood. Now, every perfection exists primarily in God, in its most perfect form, and is essentially in God. Fatherhood, therefore, exists in its utmost perfection in God. He is the Father by excellence. Being such, He cannot neglect His children. He has made them for Himself, for He could make them for none other; and He has given them the hearts of children which yearn for Him.

It is, therefore, an absolute impossibility that God could have neglected the human race; and a revelation from God, in man's present condition, is an absolute necessity. The nature of the case, and the conviction of man's mind, as evidenced by his history, all go to show this truth. What that revelation should be, or how it should be made, that is quite a different question. The main fact stands that a revelation, or communication between God and man, was necessary from the very nature of the case.

Again, God is not only a father, but the omnipotent Creator and Ruler of the universe. From these two characters and powers of God result:

First; that He could not lead astray His children, or allow them to be led astray against their will, in such a manner, that is, that, being willing and desirous to know God and serve Him, man could not only not find the way, but must go in the wrong direction. Secondly; that God has the perfect control of nature; and, after creating it, holds it in His hand, regulates its movements, wills and carries out the laws by which it is governed. No animal was ever so under the control of its master, as nature is under the control of God. Human reason teaches us this.

It follows from these two facts—that God cannot let men be led astray despite himself, and that He is the absolute Master of nature—that nature must obey Him and does obey Him; moreover, that man, being acted on by sensible things, and therefore through natural objects around him, God must make use of these objects to act upon him and raise His mind to higher things—to Himself, in fine—and cannot allow these natural objects to be the means of misleading him, if he does not wish to be misled. For did God permit nature to lead man from Himself to follow a false system of worship, that action would be imputable to God; it would argue imperfection in God, and destroy the very idea of God, which is Sovereign Perfection. Here, then, is the sure basis of communication with God; upon this must and will rest all revelation made to man. It is useless to enquire whether man needs it; his history, a history of error from the time man strayed away from God, shows he needs something more than his own feeble mind. He needed it from the beginning, and from the beginning he had it. God spoke to man through nature. Not only did He make him acknowledge his Creator by the display of His power in the elements ; He made use of nature, suspending its laws, the most familiar and necessary laws, so as to convince man that He was there, and that His Voice was to be heeded, His revelation was to be accepted. He wrought miracles ; and miracles, wonderful works which involved the suspension of nature's laws in a most marked and unmistakable manner, convinced man of God's Presence, of His work, of the truth of the words he heard, of the necessity of submission to the commands given him. A miracle was not and is not an abstract or subtle matter few can fathom. It was and is a fact ; a fact patent to all ; a fact the truth or falsity of which could and can be detected easily ; a fact witnessed by several and determined by the laws of evidence.

But before I go more deeply into this matter, let me say a word with regard to the relation between science and revelation. Science, as here taken, is the study of physical nature, carried on and systematized through the process of induction. It rises no higher than nature, belongs to it ; for it is the child of nature. This being so, it must partake of all the attributes, essential qualities of nature around us, which has been made by God. God being infinite perfection, it is impossible for nature to contradict God; for otherwise God would be a vastly imperfect God—a God of contradictions—an absurdity. In the supposition, therefore, that God made a revelation to man, He being the God of truth, his creation could not contradict His word. There must be harmony between God's words and His works. It may be difficult for a finite mind to solve the problems which would seem to show want of agreement between the Word of God as revealed, and the facts of physical science; but an agreement there is, and he is wise who, in obedience to the dictates of his own mind, which tells him he is capable of erring, does not trust what seems to him true, when he knows revelation teaches the contrary; but, instead, waits to be rewarded with the explanation further experience is apt to produce. There are a host of superficial observers and thinkers in these days, whose disposition is to war against revealed religion. The mere appearance of contradiction between science and revelation is enough for them; and, with a

cry of triumph, they hurl their assumptions in
the face of all the world has held sacred.
There are great names, on the contrary, who
have not followed this style of thought and
action. Leibnitz, Carpenter, Faraday, men of
great mind, and scientific men, of whom the
world is proud, believed in the existence of
God and of His revelation, and did *not* see
contradiction in His works and words. The
learned Abbé Moigno, of Paris, still living, is a
credit to science, and the editor of a scientific
review of value. The late Jesuit Father Secchi, the originator, I may say, of the modern
science of the physical constitution of the sun,
through the study of its spots, rose-colored
flames, and the striated lines of the spectro-
scope, was a devoted disciple of science and an
exemplary priest. The Catholic Church herself, the great bulwark of revelation, is devoted to science, and has done more for it
than those who have cast aside her control;
and it was a mark of honor the Commission of
the World's Fair, held in Paris in 1867, conferred on her when, by the hand of the Emperor Napoleon III., it placed on the breast of
Father Secchi the first prize of merit for his
scientific excellence and mechanical inventions

in meteorology. Nor is this all. The very first Academy of Science, which antedates by far those of Paris and Berlin, was founded in Rome, in the year 1603, under the name of the "Lincei," or Lynxes. In the year 1740 Pope Benedict XIV. gave it new life and a new name, calling it the "New Lynxes," and prescribed for its study natural history and experimental physics. Pius VII., in the beginning of the century, did much for it, and wished that the study of religion and of science should go hand-in-hand. It was also befriended and aided by Leo XII. Pius IX. established its seat on the Capitoline Hill, in the Capitol itself, recast its statutes and assigned it a revenue of $1,200 per annum, and gave it charge of the astronomical observatory at the Capitol. During my residence in Rome I was a witness of what these two observatories of the Capitol and of the Roman College were doing for the advancement of science.

It is, therefore, idle to assert the antagonism of science and revelation. Solid, serious science the Church patronizes and encourages, as much as she discountenances flippant science, quick in its assertions and unfair in its dealings. Bacon has taught that a philosopher must get rid of the *idola*, or idols, in his mind or feelings, before he can become a true investigator ; and these disciples of science would do well to follow this counsel of the Father of modern inductive science, and get rid of their prejudices and preconceived notions. Only by laying aside these will they be fitted to cross the threshold and enter the temple of true Science, the handmaid of God, who there proclaims His glory.

Turn to the men of solid scientific culture who to-day are listened to with respect by all, because of the vastness and solidity of their knowledge, and for the sober manner in which they treat important questions. You will not hear the satirical remark at the expense of religion. Some may have lost their belief in Christianity, but they love the truth and are not afraid to speak it. Professor James D. Dana, of Yale College, the accomplished author of the *Manual of Geology*, so highly esteemed, takes as his motto the words of Juvenal : "Nunquam aliud natura, aliud sapientia dicet"—Nature and wisdom will never contradict each other. In closing his remarks on the Progress of life, he uses these weighty words : "For the development of man gifted with high reason and will, and thus made a power above nature, there was required the special act of a Being above nature, whose supreme will is not only the source of natural law, but the working force of nature herself." In a note he distinctly asserts that there is no discordance between what he has observed and the Biblical account of creation. He further reminds his readers that the order and system made manifest in nature by geological science, leading up to ultimate perfection of all in man, is by no means atheistic, but is the only view consistent with the Divine origin of the uni-verse; and each discovery of the connection between grades of living species demonstrates still further the completeness of the system and order, and hastens its thorough under-standing.

Another writer, Mr. Le Conte, of the University of California, Professor of Geology and Natural History, in his remarks on the cal-culation of geological time, and particularly in reference to the time man has been on earth, says that geologists have "no certain knowledge" on this point. He, however, re-fers to calculations, based on the formation of deltas and on the progressive erosion of lake-

shores, which have given moderate results :
seven thousand and ten thousand years. These
are mere calculations, subjected to the vicis-
situdes of human reasoning, based on facts
which, however probable, may not be exactly
as observed or surmised. This present calcu-
lation, however, of seven, or even eight, thousand * years for the life of man on earth does
not conflict with the opinions of Catholic theologians. The Church has given no definitions
with reference to time, geological or simply
chronological, although she has given most
precise definitions with regard to facts. There
is no danger of her definitions ever clashing
with the facts of science. Once she is satisfied
that what is asserted by scientific men to be a
fact is really such, she will accept it, and interpret the Sacred Books in accordance with it ;
for it is one of her cardinal teachings that
God cannot contradict Himself, and that for
this reason His revelation and His works
must say the same thing.† From her very
teaching, therefore, on this point she must accept the fact. These facts, however, I may
state, form no part of the deposit of faith,

* Malloy grants about eight thousand as possible.

† Vat. Council, Constitutio Dogmatica, ch. iv., De Fide et Ratione.

and cannot be the subject of religious teaching.

Having thus put before you the relation of revelation to science, I return now to the ground upon which the existence of revelation rests, and from which I digressed to give you the explanation just had. That ground is the occurrence of miraculous events evidencing the interference of the Deity. It is one thing to recognize the necessity of a revelation from God, and the impossibility of nature and revelation contradicting each other; it is another thing to recognize the true revelation itself; that is a practical matter, and it is, at least ordinarily, to be compassed in a practical way. The multitude of religions in the world, with such conflicting claims, with such opposing and even contradictory teachings, makes it absolutely necessary to have some way to recognize the truth; otherwise it will be as if there had been no revelation at all. Some lull themselves into a false security by saying that enough truth exists in each one of these religions to make man good and aid him to find God. But they do not understand that the truth they recognize in each one of these systems is only some partial tradition, or the glimmer of human reason, which, as we have seen, is capable of recognizing the existence of God and the principal duties of man toward God and toward his neighbor. That is not and cannot constitute a revelation. The revelation which comes from God must be of such a kind that it exclude everything erroneous from its teachings ; for it is the word of God, who cannot teach error, cannot deceive. Secondly, it must teach all the truth that will lead man to God, keep him united to the Author of his being, and make him so live as to obtain his highest reward ; and, for this reason, it must not only teach the doctrine needed for this, but it must supply the means. Now, we have seen, in speaking of the various religions of the world, exclusive of the Christian and Jewish dispensations, as is well known from history, that these various religions, to use the words of the Apostle, "detained the truth of God in injustice" ; that is, kept the truth about God, which reason has, involved in error and in evil-doing. Why, even the moral teachings of those whose authority I have been hitherto citing, Socrates, Plato, and Aristotle, are to be censured for the error they contain. Therefore, these religions are not to be trusted, are worthless in themselves; though those holding to them may, by the light of reason, be eventually led to the truth. Moreover, the knowledge of what is to constitute truth and purity must come from God, since men are so conflicting in their views; and for this reason *there must be a practical, unmistakable manner of recognizing God as revealing to us His truth and law.* Miracles, therefore, are necessary to open man's eyes to revealed truth. There is no other way; and this is the judgment of the human race, as I have said.

A miracle may be defined to be an extraordinary event, falling under the observation of the senses, of a wonderful character, beyond the order of all created nature, and suspending nature's ordinary laws, evidently and directly attributable to the act of God Himself, done for a purpose, made known from the circumstances and worthy of Him.

This definition excludes all signs and wonders which may, through God's permission, be wrought by an agency above nature, through hidden natural laws yet unknown to us. It excludes all signs and wonders which are marvellous and, it may be, miraculous, but not

clearly so. It excludes all signs and wonders
which tend to lead men astray from the
known truth of God. It includes all those
events which so suspend nature's known
laws as to make man at once understand he
is face to face with his Maker, speaking to
him, or manifesting His presence. Such events,
for example, are those which involve the suspension of ordinary laws necessary for the
maintenance of human life, the neglect to
observe which would destroy life. Thus, to
drink a virulent poison like prussic acid, to
walk over a precipice, to cast one's self into
the sea in order to walk upon the water, such
things are fatal. To do them does or may
destroy life. Also, the immediate restoration
to health, under certain conditions science cannot explain, may be such as to cause it to be
attributed to some agency above nature, good
or bad; the end, and purpose, and circumstances will enable us to determine which;
for if it makes us love God and keep His
law more faithfully, it is from Him, and not
wrought by an agency in opposition to Him,
yet by His permission.

The purpose, moreover, for which a miracle
is wrought must, as a rule, be evident from

the circumstances or surroundings, and must
be also worthy of God.* The absence of such
a purpose is enough to make us doubt, and
even exclude a wonder or sign as coming
from God. Much more shall we exclude it,
when the purpose for which it is wrought
would tend to foster what is against God or
against the well-being of nature, by inculcating vice or by keeping men in superstition.

It is clear, then, that if we really have such
an evidence of God's action, there is *a true
miracle*, God is there; and if the act is done
to confirm His word, men will look upon the
revelation as coming from God; and this, in
consequence, essentially, of man's mental and
moral nature. So true is it, that were anything, supported by such testimony, suppos-
ably not true, God would lead man necessarily
into error, and man would not be responsible.

* Our Lord Himself gives us a criterion whereby to judge of a miracle.
In the fifth chapter of the Gospel of St. John, v. 36, we read: "The works
which the Father hath given me to perfect; the works themselves, which
I do, give testimony of me, that the Father hath sent me." Again, chap. x.
37: "If I do not the works of my Father, believe me not." 38: "But if
I do, though you will not believe me, believe the works." The works of
the Father, of God, must lead to God, to Himself; this is a mark which
must intrinsically belong to what comes from God. The absence of such
influence must make us doubt about what is said to be miraculous. Anything that leads us from God, and makes us slaves of superstition or of
passion, has the evil mark on it, is not of God, and therefore not a miracle,
however wonderful it be.

The only questions to be decided are: 1. Are miracles possible? 2. Did miracles ever occur?

Both these questions are answered in the negative by a very large class of men of science. The affirmative answer to them, however, is in the records of the past.

The Bible is a true history, the most authentic ever written. That its thousands of facts have, not only not been shown to be false, but, as far as collateral research has gone, from the earliest days of Biblical study to the discovery of the tiles in the Library of Assurbanipal by George Smith, have been proven true, is enough to make the authenticity of the Bible as clear as the noonday sun. And when we consider the theory of chances, the theory of permutations, the millions upon millions of chances of these thousands of facts not being put in such order as to coincide with historic truth, unless the Scripture narrative was based on authentic accounts, received from eye-witnesses or persons existing at the time they occurred, it is a demonstration of the historic truth of the Bible. I take but one of the Bible miracles, the Resurrection of Jesus Christ foretold by the prophet, typified in the history of Jonas and the monster of the deep,* and predicted by Christ Himself. Here we have a prophecy. Centuries before, just as the birth of Christ and the appearance of His star is foretold by Balaam, the Resurrection is predicted, for "God will not let His Holy One see corruption." We have also a prophetic fact: Jonas thrown into the sea, carried in the body of the fish for three days, and on the third day thrown up on dry land. And here let me make one *remark. Some* scientists would deny: 1. The possibility of Jonas being so swallowed; 2. The possibility of a man living under such circumstances. Now, these denials cannot stand. All things not intrinsically repugnant are possible with God, and the great monsters of the deep are not so long extinct but some one of them may not have existed at the time, and been expressly used by God for such purpose. That is certainly not intrinsically repugnant, and therefore it is possible. Further, the same scientists would have no difficulty in admitting that a person may remain cataleptic for days, giving no sign of life, not even tarnishing a mirror held to his mouth.

* דג *dag,* Hebrew text—*piscis,* a fish.

Therefore Jonas could, in some extraordinary manner, have been preserved, though under ordinary circumstances he might have died. Moreover, being alive, he resisted, as living tissues will, the action of what would otherwise have destroyed him. There is, for this reason, nothing intrinsically repugnant in the fact as narrated in the Book of Jonas.

Now, this fact was intended by the Founder of Christianity, by Him who made "the blind see, the deaf hear, the dumb speak, and the lame walk," as a fact which prefigured His Resurrection, which He Himself foretold; for He said: "As Jonas was three days in the belly of the whale, so will the Son of Man be three days in the bowels of the earth." He was put to death. His death was officially ascertained, and for that reason His legs were not broken, as were those of the men crucified with Him. To make assurance doubly sure, He was pierced with a lance in the chest from below and upward, and the broad head of the lance could not but sever the great vessels. So wide was the wound that the hand could be put into it, as the Evangelist records. He was taken down from the cross, embalmed, and buried. A guard was put at the tomb, and the tomb was officially sealed. On the third day He rose again; the tomb opened, and the affrighted guards were paid to say that, while they were asleep, the disciples came and stole away the body. "Truly," says the satirical St. Augustine, "you make use of witnesses that were asleep." For forty days He was seen by hundreds, taught and eat with His disciples. The matter could not be gainsaid. It had been foretold; it took place; it converted the world. It withstood every assault from that day. Amid all the jeers and persecutions heaped on them, the Christians looked to this astounding miracle as the proof of their revelation. They painted on the walls of their catacombs the story of Jonas; and when they were threatened with death, they raised their eyes to it, professed their faith in the Resurrection of the Son of God, and looked for a like resurrection for themselves.

From that day to this miracles have never ceased; and though not needed so much, perhaps, as then, they still occur to silence the scoffer, and to lead souls to embrace the truth of the Gospel. I am not speaking wildly.

My words may sound strangely to some one
here ; but I speak the truth, and am able to
sustain my assertion with facts. I shall mention one, which will serve for the conclusion
of this lecture.

THE CURE OF PIERRE DE RUDDER.

About fourteen years ago, a man, by name
Pierre de Rudder, of Jabbeke, near Bruges, in
Belgium, had his leg broken by the fall of a
tree. For seven years he suffered from this
fracture, which was complicated with an external wound, continually discharging. Seven
different physicians visited him ; everything
tried was of no avail. The limb shrivelled,
and dangled perfectly useless ; and walking,
without crutches, was impossible. Not only
was this the case, but on the 7th of April,
1875, he was obliged to put on the wound
an oak-bark plaster to destroy the worms in.
it. The foot could be bent from side to side,
and turned so that the heel was in front. On
that day Pierre de Rudder, who had been de-
voutly praying to Our Lady of Lourdes, visited her sanctuary at Oostakker, near Ghent.
The journey by rail and wagon caused him

a great deal of suffering, but he still continued hopeful and praying. After a while he
seems to have lost consciousness; for he
found himself at the foot of the altar, not
knowing how he came thither. He looked
for his crutches. He had left them at his
place on the bench. He rose up bewildered;
found he could stand; that he was cured
completely. He left his crutches with a religious whom I have seen and spoken to about
this case, and who has charge of the chapel
on *the* grounds. He then returned home to
Jabbeke, and on that night, April 7, 1875,
was seen walking about by two hundred people. I have myself been to this place; have
seen this man, Pierre de Rudder, and reliable
persons there. No doubt is possible. The
fact is true, and just as narrated.*

Here, then, is a modern miracle no one can
gainsay. It is an answer to the jeer that
"signs do not follow those who believe."

To sum up, my dear friends, what I have
been saying this evening, there must be a relation between God and the soul; God's char-

* See extended account in the Appendix, by the author, which was published in 1878.

acter as Father will not allow Him to leave His children without guidance. That guidance can be had only by revelation ; and the revelation God gives can never conflict with His works, or be contradicted by them, for in that case God would be a God of contradiction. The revelation the Christian accepts does not conflict with science, as scientific men themselves have admitted and do admit. The Catholic Church herself patronizes science. She was the first to establish a scientific academy. The only question, therefore, is, On what ground shall a man accept this revelation the Catholic Church claims to have from God ? The answer is : On the authority of miracles, which have made Christianity triumph over the gods of paganism, and which continue, at this day of ours, to show that God is with His own to save them from the darkness of the world, and bring them to light eternal. May all open their eyes to that light ! May the revelation of Jesus Christ be a light unto the nations. May our own people turn with disgust from the attacks made upon that revelation ! May they lay aside that spirit of levity which encourages the enemies of faith ! May they look upon the assailants of God and of His revelation as their own greatest foes, who would seek to rob them of their birthright, the loss of which means exclusion from the kingdom of Heaven—for ever—for ever!

LECTURE IV.

REVELATION, the necessity and existence of which, my dear friends, we have seen, is accepted, taken hold of by us through the assent of the intellect believing. To believe means to accept by our intellect and will any truth on the authority of another. We believe the news of the day on the authority of reliable channels; we have not seen the facts nor verified them for ourselves. We accept them because we have confidence in those who inform us. This is the essence of belief, to accept on the authority of others. The ordinary phrase, seeing is believing, is inccrrect, inasmuch as to see a thing or fact is to receive it on the authority of our own senses, and not on the authority of another. To see and to know are not, therefore, equivalent to belief or to faith.

Belief or faith is twofold, human and divine, according as our authority is human or divine; divine authority begets divine faith, human authority begets human faith. The acceptance of revelation takes place by means of divine faith, not only because we accept it on account of the character of Him who gave it, but also because the doctrines it teaches are beyond the comprehension of reason, and to accept these involves an influence on our will such as to bring our intellect into subjection to the teaching of revelation; and this can be the work of God alone, as it is not in human nature to give such obedience. Reason, however, recognizes the power of God in nature, and the existence of many things in nature it cannot explain; as, for example, the subtle work of chemical combination, the distribution of color in plants, the action of mind on matter, and of matter on mind; all these are inexplicable, but we see the facts before our eyes. It is, therefore, according to reason to imagine that God, in His infinite wisdom, can communicate to man something of what is in His Divine intellect, which far transcends the powers of the finite, weak intellect of man. To find mysteries, therefore, in revealed religion is not against reason, but, on the contrary, in accordance with it. I may go further still, and say that the existence of mysteries is postulated or demanded by reason, in such a way, that the absence of what is above reason, or of mysteries in revelation, would be a mark that it is purely human.

This divine revelation, therefore, must be accepted by divine faith or belief; and this divine faith is divine not only because the objects of it come from God, but because it is a gift from Him. Before, however, I proceed to explain what faith is in itself, and how it is a gift of God, it is necessary to say a word regarding the source, the principal source at least, of the arguments by which these truths are clearly shown; that is to say, I must first show you in what way we are to use the Bible. The Bible is used, firstly, as an historical book, a truly authentic record of facts. Those facts and collateral testimony prove the existence of a revelation of God, and show us what is the constitution of the Church of God; how it exists in this world as His representative; how it speaks in His name; how it defines truths as dogmas; how it must do this, or contradict this authentic record itself. Then, when we have thus shown what this Church of God is, we are prepared to exercise our act of faith. Up to this point the whole matter has been one of investigation which has convinced us of the existence of God's Church. Now, as faith is the acceptance of the truth or of facts on the authority of another, to have faith we must accept the authority of God residing in His Church, and it is here our divine faith begins; we believe in the Church of God, because God, who can neither deceive nor be deceived, is with it. We believe no one else with divine faith; not the Bible, nor an angel from heaven, do we believe in with divine faith, unless the Church bids us do so;* and *then* we accept the Bible, and any other truth, because the Church, speaking in the name of God and by His authority and assistance, tells us to do so.

Let us see now what this authentic record, the Bible, tells us about the Church of God. It presents to us Prophets, Apostles, Christ Himself, speaking of the kingdom of God on earth. The Prophets foretell the existence of this widespread dominion of God with men,

---

* The following words of St. Augustine are to the point: "Evangelio non crederem nisi me Ecclesiæ Catholicæ commoveret auctoritas"—"I would not believe the Gospel if the authority of the Catholic Church did not move me." (Contra Ep. Manichæi quam vocant Fundamenti, No. 6.)

which is to extend from the rising of the sun
to the going down of the same; the offering
by it to God of a clean oblation; the coming
to it of all the peoples of the earth; its position in the world as the illuminator of the human race.. The prophecies are fulfilled. The
Prince of Peace, the Father of the Age to
come, appears among men. His doctrine is
recorded. His words are unmistakable. He
abrogates the old dispensation; He establishes
the new law. He gives His commands to His
Apostles, whom He has selected, and trained,
and instructed: "Go, teach all nations; baptiz-
ing them in the name of the Father, and of
the Son, and of the Holy Ghost." "Behold, I
am with you all days, even to the consummation of the world" "I will send to you another Paraclete, the Spirit of Truth, who will
abide with you for ever, and bring all things
to your mind whatsoever I have said to you."
The Presence of God with the Church, illumi-
nating, ruling, and aiding it, is here most
clearly taught; and the absence of this note
would argue a false pretension to be the
Church of God. The Apostles, by their practice, show us how they understood their Master. They taught in the name of God. They

not only alluded to their being sent to preach;
but, with a boldness that had been blasphemy,
had it not come from the truth, they used the
formula: "It hath seemed good to the Holy
Ghost and to us." And that formula has
been religiously preserved and used in successive ages by one Church, and by one Church
only, down to the days of the Vatican Council,
when it re-echoed anew in the council-hall of
St. Peter's at Rome. Here, then, is the authority which is requisite for faith—God
speaking through His Church on earth. And
this authority is the essential foundation postulated for faith, without which faith cannot
exist.

But, some one may suggest, is there no
faith outside the Catholic Church? Can no
one have faith, unless he believe in the Church
of Rome? I will answer the objection fairly,
before proceeding farther. And my first pro-
position is, that faith and private judgment
are contradictory, and logically cannot exist together; and I think, when I explain the matter, you will agree with me also. What modi-
fications truth requires, I will make in the se-
quel. But the principle introduced in the sixteenth century by those who attempted to

reform the teachings of the Catholic Church of Rome—private judgment—is destructive of faith. Recall what I said in the beginning: faith is the acceptance of truth on the authority of another. St. Paul defines faith to be "the substance of things hoped for, the evidence of things unseen." From the nature of the case, the objects of faith are not in our possession; they are not present, they are *hoped for;* moreover, they are *unseen.* What is hoped for, what is unseen, we must take on the authority of the one who tells us of them, who has seen them, who knows they exist. Therefore this authority is essential to the act of faith. Now, my dear friends, what does private judgment say? Its language is well known to you: "I will see for myself; I accept no man's authority; I will be my own interpreter. I will see for myself what Christ taught, and that only will I hold to; there shall be no one to come between me and the Founder of Christianity." Is not this the style of speech you recognize as that of private judgment? Now mark attentively what follows from this assertion, so unmistakably clear. Use your private judgment; what results? You do not only omit to exert that legitimate, proper act of private judgment, which consists in examining the claims of Church authority on your obedience, and, those claims once recognized, surrendering, in a reasonable manner, your intellect and will to the guidance of God speaking through the Church; you absolutely, from the very outset, scout those claims as vain assumptions, and you set up in their place your own intellect and reason as judge in matters of faith. In other words, *you believe no one, no authority, trust no one but yourself;* and, therefore, your convictions are simply the result of the workings of your own mind. Yours is *conviction*, not *faith;* a natural *act*, not a supernatural act; there is no faith in *it*, because there is no acceptance of truth on the authority of another.

It results, further, that, in following private judgment, you set up a judge liable to be mistaken, a judge by no means infallible; and knowing this, you of necessity deny infallibility in matters of faith; and not only do you deny infallibility in matters of faith, but, denying even the possibility of it, you ridicule those who pretend to have it. To indulge a little pleasantry at the expense of the Catholic Church, because she teaches that she is infallible, is, as you are aware, quite in the fashion. And yet infallibility in the teaching authority of God's Church is an absolute, essential requisite to faith. Faith cannot exist without it. And as faith cannot exist without it, so is it easy to demonstrate the necessity and existence of this first requisite—infallibility—in the teaching authority. You will here, no doubt, object that I am going too far in making such a sweeping charge, that faith in no way exists among those outside the union of the Catholic Church who follow the system of private judgment: the very character of such a charge, admitting no exception, proves it groundless. And yet I maintain fully what I have said; making exception where in justice it must be made. For I do acknowledge that there is to be found faith amid the communions outside of the Catholic Church. That faith, however, so existing, is not the result of private judgment; it is the result of tradition in families, which has led many to accept revelation on the authority of those who went before, unquestioningly. That tradition has led them to look on the Bible as the word of God; to look, therefore, to the Bible, and to the Bible only, as the source of all truth about God. It is belief in the Bible, not private judgment, which constitutes their faith in God's work on earth. As long as such belief lasts, faith is possible. Sometimes, however, the assertors of private judgment use their private judgment on the Bible itself as a book. This has become more frequent of late, and with terrible result; with the result of depopulating churches, creating a generation of sceptics and unbelievers, liberalizing revealed religion, and placing in pulpits men who deny the Godhead of our Lord and Saviour Jesus Christ, Christianity itself. Private judgment, consistently carried out, has produced such men as the popular infidel lecturers of the day. *The multiplication* of these enemies of revelation puts in peril whatever of faith exists outside the Catholic Church. The recent revision of the Bible, too, is likely to give a still further shock to the faith yet existing outside the Catholic Church. For how can people look on the Bible as they once did? Shake their faith in a part, and they will begin to doubt about the rest. The existence of any faith in the religious bodies outside the visible communion of the Catholic Church is in spite of the principle of private judgment; unconsciously they are all the time accepting the authority of the tradition which tells them the Bible is true; and they do believe piously, and often in such a way as to save their souls. Being in good faith, they hold to the doctrines taught in the Bible, as far as they know them, and, living up to them earnestly, God rewards them for it. The moment, however, they begin to doubt, and fail to follow up the doubt, and find the truth, that moment they put themselves in the wrong, they remain in their bad faith; and saving faith with them, while in that state, is no longer possible.

It is really surprising, my dear friends, notwithstanding the widely-diffused teaching and practice of private judgment, that any such doctrine could ever for a moment have found favor. What is man, that he should set up his puny intellect against God? Look at the Bible itself, which not private judgment, but the care and approbation of the Catholic Church, has preserved to man as the embodiment of revealed truth to a great extent, and see what it tells us. It tells us that there existed a teaching authority in the old dispensation, which taught, in the name of God: "The Scribes and the Pharisees are seated on the chair of Moses; all things whatsoever they shall say to you, observe and do" (Matt. xxiii. 2). So spoke Christ. The Wise Men who came from the East to adore the Infant Messias, went to Jerusalem and asked of Herod where the Christ should be born. Herod consulted the priests, the guardians of the law, and the answer they gave was the true one: "In Bethlehem of Juda." There the Wise Men found the object of their search. There was, therefore, in the Old Dispensation a true teaching authority, and, by believing in it, faith was exercised and man received grace. Are we, to say that the New Dispensation was to be inferior to the Old in this respect? Was it to be a backward step, instead of a progress to greater perfection? Was God to appear to man in so special a way, as He had never done before, for so little? to do less than He had done before? The answer reason gives is: It cannot be so. God came to introduce a more perfect system in every particular, and to give greater certainty to those who believed, and a purer, higher, and surer guide, who would lead man to the certain knowledge of all He wished to teach him. This is evident from the words of Christ. He bade the Apostles go teach ; promised to be with them ; promised the Paraclete; after having for forty days conversed with the Apostles, and taught them all that was needful for them to know to carry out His work, He sent down the Holy Ghost on the day of Pentecost, to abide with them *for ever*,* to bring to their mind all things whatsoever He had said to them. Forthwith the Apostles preached with authority in the name of God, and gave to the Church of Christ the form of definition of revealed truth, based on infallibility in the Church, which, as I have said, the Catholic Church, and the Catholic Church alone, has preserved to this day.

To accept this authority of the Church and make an act of faith, my dear friends, is no merely human action. It is a supernatural act, an act which has its beginning, and continuance, and life in the grace of God. It heightens vastly our appreciation of it to know this; to recognize that we who possess it are the privileged children of God; and the effect of this truth, well appreciated, should be to so make us realize our privilege and prize

---

* *In æternum*, Vulgate, Εἰς τὸν αἰῶνα, Cod. Vaticanus, ed. Tischendorf, vii.

it, as to glory in it, and generously live up
to it. On the other hand, the mere announcement of this doctrine, that faith is a gift of
God, should not unduly depress those who
may think or know they have it not; for
God, who is our Father, wants us all to have
it, and especially those who are here to-day,
within the reach of my voice. You all can
pray; and this first gift of prayer, well used,
can bring the further gift of faith. God, says
St. Paul, wants all to be saved and come to
the *knowledge of the truth.** But it is a serious
truth, dear friends, and it becomes us to consider it seriously, and to know the grounds
upon which this truth rests. There have been
many in the past who erred in this matter;
but I will mention but one—St. Augustine, the
great Doctor of grace. With the humility of
a great and true Christian and Saint, he did
not hesitate, for the welfare of others, to confess his error. In his book on the *Predestina-
tion of the Saints*, chapter iii., he mentions that
he had been led to think the first movements
of the mind and heart towards God came
from nature; and that God, seeing the good
disposition of the heart, came to its aid, and,

* 1 Tim. ii. 4.

bestowing grace, perfected the work and gave saving faith. One day the writings of St. Cyprian fell into his hands, and he began to read. His eye fell upon a passage commenting the words of St. Paul: "What hast thou that thou hast not received? And if thou hast received, why dost thou glory as if thou hadst not received?" Immediately he saw his mistake, and, correcting himself, taught ever after the true doctrine, that even the very first movements to God which precede faith come from grace, from God, and not from nature, which only co-operates with grace. The same truth is evident from the Scripture, and from the definitions of the Church. In the sixth chapter of St. John, our Saviour is very explicit on this point. To the Jews, who were murmuring, Christ said (verse 44): "Murmur not among yourselves; no man can come to me, except the Father, who has sent me, *draw him.*" In verse 66 of the same chapter, when He hears His disciples murmuring, and sees them scandalized at His teaching, he repeats the same weighty words: "Therefore did I say to you, that no man can come to me, unless it be given him by my Father." This drawing on the part of God is the first movement to Him; for an inanimate object remains in its place until a power from without draws it. Such is the comparison Christ makes. Men do not come until this exterior force—exterior in its origin and entity, but interior in its action—moves man's heart and so draws him to God. The definitions of the Second Council of Orange and of the Council of Trent teach the same. It results from this nature of faith that it is a gift of God, not essential to human nature, though essential to his spiritual welfare here and hereafter, as the Apostle tells us: "Without faith it is impossible to please God." * It can, therefore, once had, be afterwards lost by those who trifle with it and make a bad use of it.

That faith should be of spiritual profit to us, it is not enough, my dear friends, that we should believe in the authority of God's Church, and recognize that we are indebted wholly to God for this faith we have. To be a saving faith it must not be merely a sterile belief, but an active faith, "a faith which worketh by charity"—"Fides quæ per charitatem operatur" (Gal. v. 6). It was Martin Luther who preached, in these latter days, the

* Heb. xi. 6.

doctrine that faith alone justifies. He arbitrarily introduced into his translation the word "*alone*"; and, when asked why he did so, quoted the words of Juvenal, "Sic volo, sic jubeo, stat pro ratione voluntas"--"I will have it so, so I say it shall be; my will's the reason." This infallible guide put forward this doctrine of his, certainly not in accord with the apostolic teaching; for St. James tells us: "The devils believe and tremble"; "faith without works is dead." And St. John, 1 Ep. iii. 14, says: "He that loveth not, abideth in death." Now, the doctrine that faith without works justifies underlies the whole system of what is called the Reformation. If faith alone justifies, then the Sacraments are not necessary and do not confer sanctifying grace; and baptism is therefore a mere sign, which may be dispensed with. No one need be solicitous about the exactness of the form or about the quality of the matter. Again, there is no need of doing penance; and as for punishment of a temporal nature, in the next life, faith, alone, renders it impossible. So far did Martin Luther go in this matter that he taught, in his theory of justification, that man's sins were only cov-

,ered over, and that it made no difference what he did, provided he believed. His formula was: "Pecca fortiter, crede fortius"—"Sin stoutly, but believe more firmly," a saying which opened the door to every vice; and its results so alarmed the innovator and his theologians that they strove to find some escape from it, by saying that the proof of faith was the well-doing of the believer. How that agrees with Luther's formula, "Sin stoutly, but believe more firmly," it is impossible to comprehend. The whole system is erroneous from the outset. The only faith which justifies is the faith which shows itself by a change of heart, by a change of the will, doing good works, doing penance for sin. It is not hard to show this. Take, for example, St. Paul's eloquent words regarding faith. You find that he praises it in every instance for its effects, the good works it made its possessors do. He speaks of Abraham, and lauds his faith, and says it was imputed *to him unto justice*; why? Because, believing in God, he did God's will and was ready to sacrifice his only son, Isaac. "He staggered not by distrust" (Rom. iv. 20). His uplifted hand was about to strike the blow; "And therefore it was reputed to him unto justice" (verse 22). In the Epistle to the Hebrews, besides speaking of Abraham, he tells of Abel by faith offering a sacrifice; by faith Noe framed the ark; by faith Moses denied himself to be the son of Pharao's daughter, because he esteemed the reproach of Christ greater riches than the treasures of the Egyptians. Others he speaks of who "by faith conquered kingdoms, wrought justice, obtained promises, stopped the mouth of lions, quenched the violence of fire," all of which was the reward of a life of faith and of good works, the result of that charity which is the soul of faith.

But a greater than St. Paul has testified to the necessity and to the value of good works. Jesus Christ Himself has said: Beware of false prophets; by their fruits you shall know them; every tree that bringeth not forth good fruit shall be cut down and cast into the fire. "Not every one that saith to me, Lord! Lord! shall enter into the kingdom of heaven; but he that doth the will of my Father in heaven, he shall enter into the kingdom of heaven." The will of God has to be done by us, and the will of God is clearly laid down by His law—by that law of charity which loves God above all things and our neighbor as ourself. "On this dependeth the whole law and the prophets" (Matt. xxii. 37).

In the description of the Last Judgment, our Saviour is yet more explicit in his teaching of the necessity of a faith working by charity, of the need of good works unto salvation. The description is familiar to you. The King addresses those on His right hand: "Come, ye blessed of my Father, possess *the kingdom* prepared for you from the *foundation* of the world. For I was hungry, and you gave me to eat; I was thirsty, and you gave me to drink; I was a stranger, and you took me in; naked, and you covered me; sick, and you visited me; I was in prison, and you visited me. Then shall the just answer Him, saying: Lord, when did we see Thee hungry, and fed Thee; thirsty, and gave Thee drink? and when did we see Thee a stranger, and took Thee in? or naked, and clothed Thee? or when did we see Thee sick or in prison, and came to Thee? And the King, answering, shall say: Amen I say to you, as long as you did it to one of these my least brethren, you did it to me." The

King, on the other hand, condemns the wicked because they did not do these good works.
Certainly, nothing stronger than these words
of Christ are needed to make us understand
that the only faith acceptable in His eyes,
which justifies man, is the faith that worketh
through charity, and which is rewarded, not
because it says, Lord! Lord!—in other words,
believes—but because it does the will of God,
in the doing of good works of charity.

It is no wonder, therefore, my dear friends,
when we consider all this, to find the Apostle so enthusiastic, so to speak, in enlarg-
ing on the value of faith. For faith is that
whereby we lay hold upon life eternal, and
without it that life is absolutely lost. By
it we accept the revelation of God; by it
we learn to live in accordance with God's
law; by it we lead a life of virtue; by it
we do good works of charity to our neighbor,
available to eternal life, because we see in
every poor man Jesus Christ, and therefore
act, not through a motive of philanthropy,
but through a motive of charity, the first
and last object of which is Jesus Christ. By
leading this life of faith working through
charity, we are laying up riches for the next

life. Our motive of faith is the truthfulness of God ; He has promised, and He cannot deceive us ; and, believing in Him, we shall surely receive the reward of faith. Let us, therefore, love and cherish this faith as the greatest boon we could possess. Let us not put it in jeopardy ; let us avoid exposing it to loss or to injury by careless reading, or by listening to those who speak against it. Let us, on the contrary, take the greatest care of it, foster it, guard it from the blast and frost. Let us constantly have in our hearts and on our lips that prayer of the Apostles ; "Lord, increase our faith." In this spirit we shall certainly be blessed by God with fulness of faith here, and with its reward hereafter—eternal happiness with Him.

LECTURE V.

AMONG those who profess belief in the Divinity of Christ there is a controversy, as you are aware, my dear friends, on the subject of what constitutes the Rule of Faith. Faith comes by hearing. How are we to hear? The Apostle says we are to hear by means of a preacher sent of God. Who is that preacher? The supreme authority of the Church, teaching in the name of God and by the commission of our Lord Jesus Christ, as Catholics say; or the written word of God, and the written word alone, as interpreted by each one in the use of his own private judgment, assisted by the Spirit, as is the tenet of our separated brethren? The question is a vital one, involving the dearest interests of the human race; for upon its correct solution depends the possession of revealed truth — the one boon vouchsafed by a merciful God to the poor children of Adam in this mortal pilgrimage, to end so soon in that eternity the condition of which is dependent on the way in which we have done His will, made known to us through that one means of ascertaining it. It is, therefore, with no ordinary feelings that we should approach the examination of this point.

I begin with the opinion which claims the Bible alone as the all-sufficient rule of faith, the only teacher needful. This doctrine has always been a favorite one with all those who rose up against the received teaching; though history records that, while they claimed such a rule for themselves, they were not equally inclined to extend the privileges of private judgment to those who differed with them. Their doctrine, once started, gained favor with many; and it is now the universally received foundation of all the religious bodies among us which stand opposed to the Catholic Church. On what basis does it rest? It rests on this: that as in the Christian religion all are to be taught of God, and no one is to say; "here is God, or there is God," any sincere investigator of His written word, examining in a spirit of prayer, will receive the promised light of the Holy Ghost, whereby he may know the truth. I omit, dear brethren, dwelling at length on the faultiness of this reasoning, which, interpreting the Scripture in this manner, assumes the very point in question—the power of interpreting by private judgment; and I come immediately to the direct answer to such a claim, and say that the Bible alone cannot be the rule of faith.

The first reason which substantiates my denial is one inherent in the Bible itself. The books of the New Testament, you are well aware, dear brethren, were written some time after the Gospel began to be preached. The earliest of all, the Gospel of St. Matthew, was not written till eight years after the death of our Lord. Inasmuch as Jesus Christ bade the Apostles go teach all nations in His name, promised them the Holy Spirit, which came down on them on the day of Pentecost, with the result of the immediate conversion of five thousand Jews and Gentiles; and as He, moreover, confirmed their preaching by the signs or miracles that followed, it was natural that those who had seen the works of Christ and heard His words, and were witnesses of the verification of His promises in the Apostles, should have venerated exceedingly their teachings as dictated by God, and jealously retained them either in their original form, or in copies preserved in the various churches. These originals and first copies, known as "*exemplars*," according to the custom of the time written on parchment, were religiously preserved for centuries, and were continually copied in proportion as individual churches multiplied. There was no process for stereotyping or photographing in those days. Everything depended on the accuracy, or diligence, or good faith of the copyist. That there were copyists of bad faith is notorious to every beginner in ecclesiastical history. Thus we have the Gospel of Tatian; that of St. Luke used by Marcion; the ten false epistles of St. Paul of the same heretic. The number of errors that came from want of diligence or accuracy is simply enormous; though comparatively few as affect dogmatic teaching, as can be seen in the writings of those treating of this subject professedly. Then there was another cause of error—the difference of opinion with regard to words, their position, and their punctuation. All these various causes brought about so great a divergence in the codes, as they were called, that when, in the fourth century, St. Jerome, at the request of the learned and holy pontiff, Pope Damasus, set about the translation of the Old Testament, and the revision of the New, tried by the conflicting texts consulted by him, he gave way to his feelings and exclaimed: "Tot sunt exemplaria quot codices" —There are as many exemplars as codes; as many originals, if one may say so, as copies. This was the state of the case as regards the original text. When we come to the translations, there is another difficulty of even more moment added to the first; that is, the errors of the translators. If even in copying so many mistakes were made, what was to be expected in the process of translation? St. Jerome, the prince of translators, with all the aid thorough culture, profound knowledge of languages, especially the Hebrew, and the influence of Pope St. Damasus, could give him, still spoke unreservedly of the difficulties of his task. He tells us, what it is not difficult for us to understand, that the translator or interpreter is not gifted with the inerrancy which, by the presence of the Holy

Spirit, was the prerogative of the Apostles and Evangelists who wrote the Sacred Books. Dear brethren, it is not my purpose to shake your faith in Holy Scripture, as you will see before I close; but, I ask, what is the natural consequence of such a condition of texts, codes, and translations revealed to us by the writings of this great biblical scholar? Is it not a feeling that there is an impediment inherent in the Scripture itself, which prevents the divine, or even human, certainty that the meaning we may get out of it, as a mere book, is what was intended by the Author of it, the Spirit of God? In the supposition, which is held by so many as the groundwork of their belief, that there has never been any infallible authority to decide, and private judgment is all-sufficient, the case is simply hopeless; and it is no wonder men of intelligence, who have been educated in a prejudice against authority in matters of faith, should have ended by throwing aside all hope of certitude in this matter, and consequently all revealed religion. They were logical; but the fault which is in their first principle, in their premises, is not attributable to them, but to the so-called reformers of Christianity, who not only professedly claimed no inerrancy (though in practice they actually did), but even denied such infallibility in the Apostles themselves. Martin Luther openly preferred his own spirit and interpretation to that of the Apostles. These are his words: " Be it that the Church, Augustine, and other Doctors, also Peter and Paul, yea, even an angel from heaven, teach otherwise, yet is my doctrine such as sets forth God's glory." " Peter, the chief of the Apostles, lived and taught outside of the word of God" ("extra verbum Dei"). The same thing was openly taught by others, among whom Brentius, praised by Jewell,* affirms that "St. Peter, chief of the Apostles, and also Barnabas, after receiving the Holy Ghost, together with the Church of Jerusalem, erred." John Calvin said the same thing. He asserts that "Peter added to the schism of the Church, to the endangering of Christian liberty and the overthrow of the grace of Christ." † Much as such expressions, dear brethren, may shock us, there is nothing wonderful in this. It is really the logical result of a first denial of the authority of the

---

* Protestant Bishop of Salisbury.   † See Ward's Errata.

Holy Ghost, dwelling in Christ's Church, and speaking in His name.

Besides this general difficulty in ascertaining the truth of Scripture-teaching, which is common to every people professing Christianity, and not in communion with Rome, there are special obstacles, stumbling-blocks, in the way of each one in particular. Those which especially regard persons speaking the English language are the corruptions of the Bible-text translated in the early editions of the Bible in the sixteenth and seventeenth centuries. It has been conclusively shown that the common English version of King James differs very materially from the Vulgate. This latter, as you know, dear brethren, is the edition in use and approved by the Catholic Church. So accurate is this Vulgate version in Latin, that the learned Calvinist, Theodore Beza, whose opinions were generally taken as a guide in the King's Version, said of it : "I confess that the old interpreter seems to have interpreted the Holy Books with wonderful sincerity and religion. The Vulgate edition I do, for the most part, embrace and prefer beyond all others." Yet when we come to confront the Vulgate and the King James's Version, what do we find?

We find that on at least sixteen different counts they disagree, the Vulgate teaching, the King James's Version denying, omitting, or explaining away. These points are by no means unessential ; they embrace the Holy Sacrifice of the Mass, the essence of religion, the Real Presence, the priesthood, authority of bishops, justification, good works, and free-will, besides other important points of faith. So glaring were some alterations of the editions of the English Bible of the first period of the Established Church, that many were corrected in the edition of 1683. Among other falsifications the word *altar* of the Vulgate was made to read *temple ;* the word *priest* became *elder ;* the word *grace,* with reference both to the priesthood and to the Blessed Virgin, was translated *gift ; penance* was rendered *repentance ;* and several texts were made to read in such a way as to exclude the sense of intrinsic justification and of the necessity of works. These citations, dear brethren, are more than enough to show what insuperable difficulties are in the way of the interpreter of the Scripture, relying only on private judgment, which are inherent to the Scriptures themselves. That such an interpreter, without a guide, should attain to the real sense, the real truth of Scripture, would be as great a miracle as the descent of the Holy Ghost upon the Apostles.

Besides these inherent difficulties in the reception of the Bible as the ultimate rule of faith, there are equally weighty ones on the part of the interpreter. From what I have said of the various original texts, the Hebrew and *the Greek*, as well as of the versions, it is *evident that* only scholars of the most finished culture can aspire to a competent knowledge of the meaning of Scripture. No one will ever be able wholly to attain to such a knowledge of it. Here is a first immense difficulty. Here immediately one must begin to believe some one who went before him; for not one in a thousand can succeed of himself. Then, granting that one can finally acquire the most complete assurance of the correctness of the version, he has at most only the matter, in which he must find the spirit, from which he must extract the meaning. The difficulty of this step can be well illustrated by an example. Lawyers are well acquainted with the intricacies of interpretation of law. Scarcely has a law been framed and approved, when legal authorities go to work to examine it and determine its meaning and bearing. How often, despite the greatest care, is there not a clash of opinions? The matter has to be brought to a lawfully-constituted tribunal, and the authoritative or judicial interpretation must be laid down before the law can have its full effect. And yet this happens in matters which do not exceed the grasp of reason, in practical matters, too. We can readily understand how the difficulty must increase where the matters examined are not only abstruse, but above the reach of reason, supernatural, revealed by God, and dependent on that revelation for the extent to which they can be understood; where, moreover, there is no tribunal to appeal to; where no one is to rely for assistance on his neighbor, but, from the very tenet of his faith, must rely solely on himself, and on the light which is in him. Whence is that light to come? Is it from the mere natural intellect or from the Holy Spirit? It cannot be from the mere natural intellect; for as the object and the mode of assent to it are of an order above nature, no such disproportion can exist. Therefore it must be assisted, and the assistance must come from above. And this, in fact, is what is claimed by the advocates of private judgment in matters of faith. They tell us that the Holy Ghost is with them, and enables them to understand and derive comfort from so much of the Scripture as it may be they are moved to read and reflect on. Now, this is an assertion made without foundation in Scripture. Not only is this so, but we have facts to contradict the assertion.

You are all familiar, dear brethren, with the narrative, given us in the Acts, of the manner in which the deacon Philip and the eunuch of Queen Candace were brought together by the Spirit of God. It was precisely a case of complete failure of private judgment. The eunuch was seated in his chariot, reading a passage from the prophet Isaias; but he was not able to understand it. The Spirit of God spoke to Philip and bade him go join the eunuch. He did so, and asked the eunuch if he understood what he was reading. The eunuch replied: "How can I, unless some man show me?" Philip, at his request, did show him the meaning of the passage, and the man was converted and baptized. Here we have private judgment at fault; and, in contradistinction, the teacher ordained of God, resulting in belief, saving faith. This is, moreover, confirmed by the words of St. Paul: "Faith cometh by hearing."

But we are to judge a tree by its fruits. This principle of private judgment, since its first erection into a system in the sixteenth century, has had ample time and opportunity to develop, to put forth foliage, and bear abundant fruit. What fruit has it borne? Has it borne the fruit of that unity of belief and of will for which Jesus Christ prayed: "Holy Father, keep them in Thy name whom Thou hast given me, that they may be one, as we also are"? What is the unity of belief, what the harmony, which have sprung from private judgment? You know, dear brethren, better even than I do, the numberless divisions on the score of faith which distract Christian peoples. The very first result of private judgment in matters of faith was to produce those widely differing churches, the Lutheran, the Calvinistic, and the Anglican. Since then the process of subdivision has been going on with alarming rapidity, until now the question is, not so much to settle upon points that all must hold under penalty of being excluded from church-membership; but rather to see what mutual tenet will succeed in gathering under its banner the greatest number of men of broad views; of those, in a word, who desire to hold the least possible amount of revealed truth. It has come to this, dear brethren, that one feels relieved if he does not hear open profession of disbelief in the divinity of Jesus Christ. Nor is this all; the preaching of religion has in very many instances, and with increasing frequency, fallen into the hands of those who substitute their own excited imaginations and wild speculations for revealed truth; who speak of the Bible as, if cautiously used, well adapted to teach morality, nothing more; and these men, by the power of their eloquence and the captivation of their manner, sensational in the extreme, hold in absolute bondage those who boast of their intellect, and glory in the privilege of judging for themselves. To crown all, we have daily before us the spectacle of men and women who make themselves the priests and priestesses of spiritism, and, either dealing with powers above them or carried away by excitement, renew the scenes of bygone days, the consultations with the departed spoken of with condemnation by the inspired writer and by Fathers of the Church—a retribution on those who have left the paths marked out by revelation. And each one of these, like the pythons and pythonesses of old, is followed by a number of credulous

persons, who accept as truth whatever is said in
moments of wild paroxysm or pythonical inspira-
tion. It is a sad sight to witness, dear brethren.
It takes one back to the paganism Christ freed
us from. We seem to see the days of mental in-
fatuation of old Rome, of which St. Leo writes :
"Magnam sibi acquisivisse religionem videbatur,
quia nullum respuebat errorem." Would it were
only in imagination that we are carried back
to those days! With these aberrations we see
returning pagan maxims and pagan practice, the
supremacy and deification of the state, the loos-
ening of the marriage-tie—the very safeguard of
Christian society,—the exalting of might over
right, and of the senses over all that is spiritual
and intellectual. Even science itself feels the effects of this materialism. Our duties to God are
not the ordinary subject of the investigation of
intelligent men ; nature, what they see around
them, claims their attention and that of the people applauding ; and this not with any aim or intention of manifesting the glory of the Author
of nature, but for the purpose of chaining her
to the car of man's material progress.

Such, dear brethren, is the result of the aban-
donment of the guiding light of faith ; such is the
evil way the mind of man takes when left to it-

self.   God, who foresaw this, in His mercy vouchsafed to give us a means to avert the danger, and to have always the sure protection of which man stands in need.   For this purpose He instituted His Church, and bade His Apostles, "Go, teach in my name; as the Father hath sent me, so I send you; whosoever will not hear you, let him be to you as the heathen and the publican." Could anything clearer be needed to show the existence of authority to which the judgment of each one must yield?   That authority we see, in the *Sacred Books*, exercised not only in teaching, *but* also in making laws.   Thus, St. Paul lays down laws for the direction of Christians in public worship, excommunicates the incestuous Corinthian, and bids those who are faithful avoid those who have apostatized.   St. John speaks in like manner.   The Holy Ghost is promised and given to the Church, the Spirit of truth, "who," as Christ, in the Gospel of St. John, tells us, "will teach you all things whatsoever I have said to you" (St. John xiv. 26).   What is the consequence of this promise and its fulfilment? It is, dear brethren, this: that the Church of God is the depositary of all revealed truth, and the teacher of all truth revealed, and consequently the guardian of all that appertains to or contains it. In two founts or sources does she keep this sacred treasure, and from them does she draw it when needful—in Scripture and in Tradition; for, as the holy Œcumenical Council of Trent, in its fourth session, tells us, the Church receives and venerates both with a like feeling of piety and reverence, as divine in their origin. But the Church, dear brethren, does not seek the reason of her existence in Scripture; hers is a higher claim. As to the Scripture, she is the guardian of it. She existed before it. She came before the nations with the stamp of divine approbation on her in the first ages as it is on her now; for God confirmed her mission by making clear that He was with her, by miracles, by charismata, by the practice of the counsels of Christian perfection. Before a word of Scripture—that is, of the New Testament—was penned, the Church of Christ existed, and appeared in far-off lands; and it was verified, with regard to the Apostles, that the sound of their voice had gone forth throughout the earth. Christianity was preached, then, before the New Testament was written. Two consequences flow from this, dear brethren: first, that the ordinary way of making known the truth of God is by the preaching of the Word, God Himself, that man

may not glory, giving the increase ; second, that
the Church, in which the Holy Ghost dwells, is
the judge and interpreter of Scripture ; for to her
was it needful that the writings and teachings of
her Apostles should be submitted, in order that
the faithful might be sure they were not led
astray. St. Paul himself bears witness to this,
when he tells us he went up to Jerusalem, that
he might compare his doctrine with that of those
who were there, "lest he had run or should run
in vain." And this office of judge and guardian
of Holy Writ, in virtue of her high authority
and commission, the Church has never proved
false to. She it was who, amid the confusion of
exemplars and codes, carefully preserved what
was genuine, consecrating it by her use of it ; and
by her canon of Scripture in the Council of Car-
thage, the decrees of her pontiffs, Innocent and
Gelasius, down to the decree of the Council of
Trent (sess. iv.), vindicated the genuineness of
each of the Sacred Books and their parts. To
her, dear brethren, are you indebted for the
Bible to-day. The oldest codes of it you have
cannot claim an antiquity equal to hers ; for
they go no farther back than the fourth century, and for the most part are wanting in some
particular. As she, then, has been the faithful

guardian of Holy Writ, and has so jealously cared for it as to extort, as we have seen, the praise of Theodore Beza, and that, in virtue of her Divine Spouse assisting her; she has, too, in virtue of that same Spirit, the power of interpreting its meaning, so that it is not lawful to follow any other meaning or edition than what we know to have been approved of by her. In this way are the children of the Church providentially protected from the incubus of erroneous teaching and interpretation which oppresses those outside the Church, and prevents them from attaining to the knowledge of the truth once delivered to the saints.

But it is not alone in Sacred Scripture, dear brethren, that revealed truth is contained. Tradition, as the Council of Trent says, is to be received and venerated equally with Scripture. You are well aware how the world looks on such a doctrine. Yet it is a doctrine not only eminently reasonable, but which has its foundation in Holy Writ itself. In several places mention of traditions occur, but I cite only one, from the Second Epistle of St. Paul to the Thessalonians, ii. 15. He tells them: "Therefore, brethren, stand, and hold the traditions you have learned, whether it be by word or by our epistle." This text the English versions of 1562, 1577, and 1579 translated otherwise, rendering the word, not *traditions*, but *ordinances*. It is worthy of remark, however, that the edition of 1683 corrected this change, restoring the objectionable word *traditions*. But though the text and its history are sufficient of themselves to bring about conviction, there are arguments from facts recorded in the Bible which are conclusive of a tradition of faith, which God did not intend should be lost. The first of these I have in part alluded to already, when speaking of the interpretation of Isaias, given by the deacon Philip to the eunuch of Queen Candace, on his way to Ethiopia. Is it to be supposed for a moment that this new convert, a man of intelligence and of influence, did not remember the explanation of the prophet's words, and repeat it to his fellow-countrymen? No; that tradition remained with the people, who, notwithstanding their isolation, must have kept such tradition jealously, as they kept the main traditions of Christianity. And it is not a little singular that, among the traditions, though erroneous, which they have handed down from father to son through so many ages, there is one which favors the Immaculate

Conception of the Mother of God: namely, that her soul was created before the souls of other men—a provision, the effect of which would save her from the sin in which we are all born. But this is a digression.

I come to the second fact which proves the existence of tradition. It was the third day after the Resurrection, and two of the disciples were wending their way to the little village of Emmaus, when suddenly an unknown Person joined them. This unknown Person was none other, as you know, dear brethren, than Christ Himself; but, as the Gospel tells us, "their eyes were held that they did not know Him." And He said to them, "What are these discourses that you hold one with another, and are sad?" They replied, telling Him of what had occurred in Jerusalem, and how Christ, who, they had hoped, would have redeemed Israel, had been put to death, but was said to have arisen. Jesus Christ answers them: "O foolish and slow of heart to believe in all things which the prophets have spoken. Ought not Christ to have suffered these things, and thus have entered into His glory? And beginning at Moses and all the prophets, He expounded to them, in all the Scriptures, the things that were concerning Him." Now, here we have a most important interpretation of Scripture, given by Christ Himself, the author of our holy religion. Do you find one word of that interpretation in this place, or in any other place of the New Testament? No; there is not a word said of it beyond the fact that Moses and the other prophets did speak of Him, as in other parts of the Bible He tells us. Is it at all credible that this authentic interpretation of the predictions regarding Christ were allowed by these disciples to remain unknown? By no means; for we read that the disciples told what happened to them on the way. That interpretation was not forgotten. Every word of it was cherished and handed down, and constituted a part of that living tradition even more potent, if possible, in its influence on the life of the Church, than the Scripture itself.

The third fact I referred to is the one of which the Evangelist St. Luke tells in the first chapter of the Acts. He says that Jesus Christ "showed Himself alive to His Apostles, by many proofs, for forty days appearing to them and speaking to them of the kingdom of God." Here Christ is represented as in frequent communication with the Apostles during these forty days, and He speaks to them of His Church, of the kingdom which He had come to found on earth, which was not of this world. Yet very little is found in the Gospel of what He said. The Gospel was rather concerned in telling what He did, that the resurrection of Christ might be evident to all. What He said, except in a very few instances of the highest importance, the Bible does not tell us. It was during this time Christ explained and regulated the constitution of His Church, and the explanations and regulations remained with the Apostles, and were handed down by them, through the Spirit promised and afterwards given them to recall to their mind whatsoever their Master had said. This is further evident from what St. Luke says in the last chapter of his Gospel. Christ, when He had eaten before His Apostles and disciples, explained to them anew the words of the prophets and of the Psalms concerning Him. Yet, while mentioning the fact, the Evangelist only adds: "Then He opened their understanding, that they might understand the Scriptures." There is nothing so evident as that Christ left His Apostles a teaching body, entrusted with knowledge for others, which was not then recorded, because such record was not deemed necessary. The action of the inspired writers, with what they tell us, shows this conclusively. It is clear that this authority to teach stands in a high position over both the written and spoken word—Scripture, that is, and Tradition—to make use of the one and of the other, as the Spirit may dictate. Scripture and Tradition are the treasures entrusted to the keeping of God's Church; from these, and these alone, does she draw the doctrine she unerringly teaches. The canon of Scripture gives us the books which contain the written word of God. Tradition is contained in the writings of the Fathers and councils approved as witnesses by the Church, and in *the living* belief of the faithful, held always, everywhere, and by all. Such is the celebrated rule of St. Vincent of Lerins, laid down in his well-known work, the *Commonitorium;* and St. Augustine, too, gives us this same principle, when he says, in his fourth book against the Donatists: "What the universal Church holds that has not been instituted by councils, but has always been retained, is most rightly believed to have been handed down, not otherwise than by apostolic authority." St. Irenæus, Tertullian, and other Fathers speak in like manner in praise of Tradition.

It was with her supreme authority and with those two sources of truth, always in her charge, that the Church of God, dear brethren, set about approving and presenting to her children a faithful copy of the Scriptures. Up to the Council of Trent, there existed no edition of the Old and New Testament which enjoyed an approval of its authenticity on the part of the teaching authority of God's Church. Her practice in using the edition, known as the "Old Vulgate edition," through so long a series of centuries, was a guarantee that it contained no error against faith or morals, and that, substantially, it was the Word of God. But that it was entirely free from mistakes of words, and even of sentences, no one of learning would assert; for, as I have already said, the various readings were very numerous. The attacks made against the Church by the innovators of the sixteenth century, who each took his stand on the Bible; the facility of being led astray which came from such a variety of translations; the accurate knowledge of dead languages required to detect fraud, all convinced the Fathers of the Council of Trent that it was advisable to give the faithful an edition which would, on account of the sanction of the Church, be looked to with greater reverence, and be used with greater confidence. Therefore it was that, after approving the old Vulgate edition, rendered authoritative by the use of so many centuries, the council ordered it should be printed as free from faults as possible — "ut quam emendatissime imprimatur." This work, the history of which is full of interest, was carefully carried out under the eye of the Sovereign Pontiff, who called to his aid the most learned scholars of the Church, and had brought to Rome the most valued ancient codes he could obtain. In this way finally issued from the press the Vulgate edition now in use in the Catholic Church, the only complete Bible the Church of God ever authentically approved, no matter what its language or under what circumstances other editions may have been given to the public. This Vulgate edition the Church commands to be read in her assemblies, and puts in the hands of the faithful with the interpretations she approves. It is this edition of which she permits, through ecclesiastical authority, the translations for the private use of her children, so that every one may receive the instruction and edification it is intended to impart.

Such has been the conduct of the Church.

That conduct, instead of causing the Bible to be despised, has had the effect of causing it to be still more honored and more widely spread. In guarding the reader against the difficulties of interpretation inherent in the text itself, against those inherent in the interpreter himself, with that fulness of divine authority received from her Founder and from her Spouse, going before and showing the true sense of its Author, the Holy Ghost, she confers an immense, an incalculable benefit on mankind. Has this beneficence been gratefully acknowledged? By those in her communion it has. But with respect to those outside of her communion, this very act has been made the pretext of charges the most false, and the object of attacks the most virulent. It was, however, not unreasonable to expect such a line of conduct from those who, by such a proceeding on the part of the Church, were directly pointed out as contradictors of revealed truth. Jesus Christ came to convict the world of error and of injustice. His words and His acts merited for Him false witness, ignominy, and death. He told His followers that the disciple could not expect more leniency than fell to the lot of the Master. He told them that the world would hate them because it first hated Him.

He foretold they would be oppressed, and bade them not be discouraged, but to put their confidence in Him, for He had conquered the world. And therefore it is, dear brethren, that when we see the Church in her perennial struggle with the world—whether it be with the pagan persecutors or the barbarian rulers that enthralled her; with the innovators of the sixteenth century or the rationalistic governments of the nineteenth—we should not be either surprised or cast down. We must expect to hear her calumniated, and held up as the betrayer of the deposit she was called into being to protect and foster. What has been done by her, *dear brethren*, with regard to that deposit, I have shown you. No mother has ever watched over her child with more solicitude than she has guarded that offspring of the Holy Spirit's virtue in the souls of the Apostles—His inspired word. Not only has she saved it from harm, not only has she done all in her power to make it perfect, but she has taught *us to* reverence, honor, and love it.

Let us cherish, then, a heartfelt gratitude towards her for thus preserving to us, free from all taint, the Holy Word of God, that it might, under her guidance, be " useful to teach, to reprove, to correct, to instruct in justice." Let us, imitating her, treat it always with the reverence due it; for she puts it on the altar in her councils, and honors it daily in her liturgy. Let us read it with the docility of spirit which is the gift of the Holy Ghost; such docility will merit for us that He open our intellect to aid us to understand it, appreciate it more, and make its maxims the rule of our life. Amen.

LECTURE VI.

IN my last discourse, dear brethren, we saw that the Bible, though, as St. Paul says, "useful for teaching," cannot of itself teach, because of the need of an interpreter; because it tells us expressly to obey an authority instituted by God; and because, moreover, it does not contain all that was revealed and taught by Christ. I come now to speak of what in the Church of God is the authority speaking in His name. What is the *Ecclesia docens?* It is that body which has inherited the duties and rights given by Christ to the Apostles, to whom He said: "Go, teach all nations." That body is composed of the Head of the Church and the bishops of the Church united with the Head— the Sovereign Pontiff and the bishops. This is the body which represents Christ, to whom He said: "He that hears you hears me"; "Behold, I am with you all days even to the consummation of the world " ; " The gates of hell shall not prevail against my Church." The gates of hell would most certainly prevail against the Church, she would, in fact, be without the promised presence of Christ and of the Holy Ghost, if it were at all possible for the teaching body of that Church to present for belief to the faithful any doctrine not true. And therefore it is we say the true Church of God can teach no error, the supreme teaching authority of the Church, the Pope and the bishops united with him, in œcumenical council or otherwise, can by no possibility lay down as dogmatic belief what is not revealed; and this privilege she has from the Holy Ghost dwelling in her. This is what is known as the prerogative of infallibility. This infallibility, one in its source, is twofold in its manifestation ; it is in the Head, and it is in the Church at large united with the Head. In other words, the Holy Spirit is ever working in a double manner : in the Head to cause him to teach infallibly the universal Church ; in the bishops united with the Head to make them preserve the doctrines and traditions of the faith and instruct their flocks in them. So that, dear brethren, not only is it impossible that the Sovereign Pontiff, and the bishops with him, should ever have given or should

ever give any false *ex-cathedrâ* or official definition of dogma for the whole Church ; it is equally
impossible that the whole body of bishops of the
Catholic Church should fall away from the faith.

But though that infallibility is thus twofold in
its manifestation, it is, my dear brethren, essentially one, because its author, the Holy Ghost, is
one. The Head of the Church is infallible with
or by reason of that same infallibility with which
Christ willed His Church to be endowed. In undertaking, then, to show that the Sovereign
Pontiff is infallible in his *ex-cathedrâ* teachings,
I, by this fact, also show the infallibility of the
Church, of which undoubtedly the principal
share or part, or the chief exercise, lies with the
successor of St. Peter, the Bishop of Rome.
Around him the whole system revolves in perfect harmony ; and he alone enjoys a personal
infallibility in official teaching of the universal
Church.

It is, therefore, to the infallibility of the Sovereign Pontiff that I shall confine my remarks
to-day. I shall reserve for the next discourse
the examination of the decree of the Vatican
Council.

Every society, dear brethren, requires a head.
Order is Heaven's first law. Order is the parti-

cipation of the divine harmony given to created
nature. Everything is subordinate to God, and
in creation of intelligent beings, whom He
made to do His will, He has made it a necessity of their co-existence, as well as a mark of
His sovereignty, that there should exist among
them some supreme authority. It comes thus
from the very essence of society ; and as society
is from God, so is authority from God, as the
Apostle tells us. Now, the Church is a society,
an association for a definite purpose, it is true,
but a perfect society, not needing in itself any
other authority for its conservation, and for the
attainment of its end. It is, therefore, necessary, as is evident from what I have just said,
that it have a head. This being so, the prerogatives of that Head must spring from the nature
of the association or society. The nature of the
society which constitutes the Church of God, is
to preserve the deposit of faith, and the unity of
the fold. As for this double purpose there must
be power to teach what is contained in the deposit, and to hold the flock together by laws de-
vised to that end, inherent in that society, so its
official head must be the one to hold and exercise such power of teaching and ruling. In some
societies, it is true, the head is, as it were, merely

an executive officer, the legislation having been done by other bodies belonging to them, which for this reason are known as supreme bodies, to which are subject the executive officers themselves. But those officers, merely executive, are rather something introduced into society for purposes of prudence, than natural results of association; for the natural state of society was and is, that the supreme power lies with the head; whether this society be that of the family, or that of the original state, the result of patriarchal rule. Now, when we come to consider the Church, we find a society immutable in its form, because founded by God, and perfect in its organism. Such an origin, and the action of the Church itself, substantiate the assertion of the supreme power of its Head, and add value to the reasons I have given.

We must bear in mind always that Christ promised His Spirit to His Church; sent down upon it that Spirit, the Spirit of Truth, to abide with it for ever; and, moreover, promised to be with it to the consummation of the world. In fine, He foretold that, though it would be tried in every way, the gates of hell would never prevail against it. Hence it is impossible that this Church should ever teach false doctrine; for in that case the Spirit of Truth would not be with it, and the gates of hell would have prevailed against it—the Spirit of Truth would have departed and the father of lies would have triumphed. Wherefore, dear brethren, the highest official teaching of the Church must be received as the word of God revealed and contained in Holy Scripture and in Apostolic Tradition.

What does the official teaching authority of the Church say? What action has it taken, which will substantiate the assertion that the supreme teaching and ruling power is in the Head of the Church?

If we turn to the Œcumenical Council of Florence, held in the year of our Lord 1439, we find the Fathers, in union with the Sovereign Pontiff, defining that " the Roman Pontiff, the true Vicar of Christ, is the head of the whole Church and the father and doctor of all Christians ; and that to him, in St. Peter, was committed by our Lord Jesus Christ the full power to feed the universal Church, to rule and to guide it." What is the most natural deduction from these words? Is it not that the Sovereign Pontiff, herein declared the doctor or teacher of the Church, should possess the infallibility which belongs to the Church? The very idea of a teacher conveys this ; for a teacher is only rightly so called when he can impart that degree of certitude which is essential to what he teaches. If the science is physical, he must impart physical certainty as far as it is possible ; if it be a speculative one, he must give the metaphysical certainty which is proper to it ; if theological, the theological certainty which comes from revelation. Consequently the teacher of the universal Church must be able to impart this theological certainty, which, as I said, comes from revelation. It will not do for him to teach as subordinate teachers do. They are taught by the Church. He is the "teacher of the Church," throughout the world. Consequently, what he teaches must be known to him not from others, but by a special assistance of God ; and for this additional reason, because his act of teaching or judging is a personal act. I invite your attention, dear brethren, to this point. A supreme judge, who gives sentence, exerts a personal act ; if he do not, then he is only a simple mouth-piece, a simple instrument. But when he is a supreme judge, such as we have in our different countries, his decision is the result of his study, of his information, of his legal acumen, of his sound judgment. Therefore, such an act is eminently a personal act ;

and because it is a personal act we honor most highly, and most justly, the learned men who discharge such a difficult duty. Now, dear brethren, when we come to consider the Sovereign Pontiff in the discharge of his duty, as teacher of the Church, we see him occupied in examining, studying, praying, and judging, in order to define what the doctrine of the Church is. If he takes the decisions of the Church, the writings of the Fathers, the traditions of apostolic origin, it is that he may compare them, revolve them in his mind, and judge with respect to the question at issue. This is involved in his duty of teacher, and this is, too, an eminently personal act. Every one must judge for himself; another cannot judge for him. I may follow the judgment of another, but *my* judgment is and can be only *mine*, and no one else's. Therefore the act of the Sovereign Pontiff in judging and deciding matters of faith and morals, as supreme teacher of the universal Church, is a personal act, and he is therefore personally infallible.

This truth, which is evident from the nature of the Church, and from the position and duty of its Head, is clearly proved from Scripture and from Tradition, as contained in the writings of

the Fathers, as I shall briefly show. There are
three texts of Scripture especially which, in
showing the position of Peter among the Apostles, prove that he possessed for himself and for
his successors the prerogative of supreme infallible teaching in matters of faith and morals.

The first is that which is found in the sixteenth chapter of St. Matthew: "And Jesus
came into the quarters of Cesarea Philippi: and
He asked His disciples, saying: Whom do men
say that the Son of Man is? But they said:
Some John the Baptist, and other some Elias,
and others Jeremias, or one of the prophets.
Jesus saith to them: But whom do you say
that I am? Simon Peter answered and said:
Thou art Christ, the Son of the living God. And
Jesus answering, said to him: Blessed art thou,
Simon Bar-Jona, because flesh and blood hath
not revealed it to thee, but my Father who is in
heaven." Observe, dear brethren, the prerogative
of Peter. God Himself in heaven has deigned
to turn His eyes on him, and give him this extraordinary gift of faith—to him individually, for
Christ addressed him individually: "*Simon, son
of Jona.*" "And I say to thee, thou art Peter,
and upon this rock I will build my Church, and
the gates of hell shall not prevail against it.

And I will give to thee the keys of the kingdom
of heaven. And whatsoever thou shalt bind on
earth, it shall be bound also in heaven; and
whatsoever thou shalt loose on earth, it shall be
loosed also in heaven."

In this text, speaking to Peter, Christ fulfils
the prophetic words uttered when He called him
and said to him: "Thou shalt be called *Cephas*,
which is interpreted Peter." This name is from
the Syro-Chaldaic, the language spoken by our
Lord, the word from which it is formed signifying a *rock*.* The simile, so clear in this
place, dear brethren, cannot be misunderstood.
Nothing is so usual as this expression even
now. The foundation is everything in an edifice; if that be bad, the building will fall;
if it be rock, there is no danger. So Christ
Himself said when speaking of those who did
not build their houses on sand. What is remarkable here is that Simon, the son of Jona,
praised for his faith and open profession of belief
in Christ's divinity, is the one designated as the
rock upon which the Church is to be built. The
firmness of the rock is given him, and that
building against which the gates of hell are not

* John i. 42; Heb , בֵּף ; Syro-Chal., כֵּיפָא; πέτρα, Tischendorf ed.
vii.; "petra," Vulgate.

to prevail is to be built on that foundation, which, of course, cannot have less strength, or less permanence, than the edifice resting on it. Our Lord, with extraordinary words, promises him a power unlimited: *"Whatsoever thou shalt bind,"* etc. There is no limit put to it. He tells him, moreover, that He will give him the keys of the kingdom of heaven. It is not needful that we delay on this point. The expression is familiar to you as designating power; and so, too, the custom evidenced in Scripture of the minister of the king carrying on his person a key to represent his power, and the consequent reference to this where the exercise of power, subordinate only to the supreme ruler, is expressed; as, for instance, when the prophet Isaias says of Eliacim, the son of Helcias (Is. xxii. 22): "I will lay the key of the house of David upon his shoulder." To Peter, therefore, is promised the first place in Christ's Church, unlimited power, and firmness like that of the rock, in order that upon him may be built the Church, against which the gates of hell are not to prevail. This certainly proves the primacy of Peter, and at the same time his inerrancy; for as the Church would undoubtedly be prevailed against if it could be led astray in doctrine, so would it be prevailed against in like manner if its foundation were shaken, if Peter were to err in the exercise of his supreme teaching authority, or his power be weakened.

The second text is that which is taken from the Gospel according to St. Luke, ch. xxii. v. 31. Our Lord was partaking of the Pasch with his Apostles, and after the institution of the Blessed Eucharist, as there was a strife among them, "which should seem to be greater," * He chides them for this, and then turns to Peter, saying: "Simon, Simon, the devil hath sought *you* (*expetivit vos*) that he might sift *you* as wheat; but I have prayed for thee that thy faith fail not, and *thou*, being once converted, confirm thy brethren." These words are so clear, dear brethren, as hardly to need explanation. I only call attention to the distinction made here by Christ between the Apostles all and Peter. He says to the Apostles: The devil hath sought *you* —in the plural. To Peter he says: I have prayed for *thee* (*pro te*), that thy faith fail not; thou,

---

* Even if this discussion took place some time before, as has been said, the fact of its being introduced here is of the greatest significance; one realizes this the more he thinks about it. All editions, even those like the English version of the Polyglot; D'Oyly & Mant's, ed. 1856, which in a note says this discussion took place at this time; and Tischendorf's seventh edition, have this account, here. As Gallicanism is dead, it is time to stop making concessions to it.

being once converted, confirm thy brethren, strengthen them in their faith. The office of Peter was a future one ; he was first to fall, that he might learn his strength was not of himself, but from God. In fact, Simon Peter, stimulated by these words, makes a profession of fidelity till death ; but Christ tells him he will fall before cock-crow. Thus we see, dear brethren, that this great prerogative we claim for Peter is no inherent power of man, but a free gift of God for the good of His Church.

The third text I referred to is taken from St. John xxi. 15, seq. Peter had thrice denied his Lord. Christ causes him to declare thrice his love for Him, and replying each time He says : "Feed my lambs ; feed my lambs ; feed my sheep." The Greek word used here, ποίμαινε, having as its root the word ποίμην, signifying a shepherd, means : Feed my lambs with authority. The mode of feeding is certainly not an act of giving material food ; so that we have to understand it in a figurative sense—that is, of feeding with doctrine. It is impossible that our Lord would have given such a commission to Peter if He had not intended to preserve him from error ; especially if we take into consideration the relation this triple confession has with the triple denial, and the words which Christ used just before He predicted that triple denial: "I have prayed for thee that thy faith fail not; thou being once converted, confirm thy brethren." We shall see, dear brethren, that the tradition and practice of the Church bear out the interpretation I have given.

But before I pass to show this, I must not omit mention of a fact of apostolic practice which speaks volumes in support of the doctrine of the infallibility of Peter and his successors. St. Paul, the Apostle of the Gentiles, had received his revelation directly from God. He went into Arabia and there remained for some time, returning to Damascus. After three years he "went to Jerusalem to see Peter, and tarried with him fifteen days" (Gal. i.) He adds: "Other of the Apostles I saw none, saving James, the brother of the Lord." We see James mentioned here only incidentally; Peter is the great figure presented, the one he went to see. Why? The reason, if doubtful after what I have said, is evident from another passage of St. Paul, chap. ii. He tells us: "Then after fourteen years I went up again to Jerusalem." Peter's name does not occur here, either because he was not in Jerusalem, or because the Cephas mentioned here is he. The point is a disputed one ; but granting that Peter is here meant, we find St. Paul conferring with "James and Cephas and John," "lest perhaps I should run or had run in vain." The subjection of an Apostle to the supreme teaching authority in the Church, as openly declared here by him, dear brethren, should serve as a most convincing argument to those who are tempted to follow their own judgment in pre ference to its declarations, and make us who believe appreciate more thoroughly the august character of the authority vested in Peter and his successors.

That the primacy of Peter, as shown by these texts, was not only accepted by the universal Church from the beginning, but primarily because of the inerrancy of Peter's successors and inheritors of the promises made to him, is to be seen from the writings of the Fathers, of whom I shall cite only a few.

St. Irenæus * was a father of the second century. He was a disciple of St. Polycarp, Bishop of Smyrna, who had been a disciple of St. John the Apostle. He was in a condition, therefore, not only to know facts, but also the ideas and feelings of apostolic times. What do

* Euseb. v., H. E., c. 24.

we find him saying and doing? In his work
against heresies he tells us of St. Peter and St.
Paul founding the Church at Rome. He himself
comes to Rome, sent by the clergy of Lyons to
St. Eleutherius, Pope, in the case of the Mon-
tanist heresy; just as his master, Polycarp, had
come to Pope Anicetus to treat of the celebration of Easter. This is not all; in the third
chapter of his third book he has these remarkable words: "Pointing to the tradition of the
Church founded and constituted at Rome by
the most glorious Apostles Peter and Paul, we
confound all those who in any way, through
self-complacency or vainglory, or through
blindness and ill-will, gather other than they
should. For to this Church, on account of its
more powerful principality, it behooves every
church to come—that is, the faithful everywhere." He goes on to designate the successors of Peter. What is even more, he tells us
that St. Clement, who was the successor of St.
Peter, although the Apostle St. John was still
alive, was the one to write to the Corinthians,
among whom contention had arisen, to settle
their disputes. Later on we have St. Cyprian,*
who speaks of the unity of the Church, saying:

* For letter of St. Cyprian, see Alzog, *Church History*, § 87, vol. i.

"The beginning is from unity, and the primacy is given to Peter, that the Church may be shown to be *one*." Whence is this unity to flow, dear brethren, if inerrancy of faith is not the source, and therefore the reason, of the primacy?

St. Jerome was a father of the fourth century. He was in his prime about the year 270, with all the advantages of having lived in the centre of Catholic unity. He left Rome for the East, and he was then, at the time of which I wish to speak, at Antioch. He found himself in the midst of the excitement consequent on the discussion concerning the personality and natures of Christ. The Bishop of Antioch wished him to subscribe to a formula in which the word *hypostasis* occurred in the sense of substance. The term was equivocal, some understanding person, others substance. St. Jerome * writes with great earnestness to Damasus, then ruling the Church of Rome. He begs him to let him know which he is to use—the term three *hypostases* or only one. He says: "I, following none other but Christ, am joined in communion with your beatitude—that is, with the cathedral of Peter; I know

* Epist. St. Hieronym., l. l., ep. 35.

that the Church has been built on that rock.
Whosoever eateth the Lamb outside this house
is profane. Whoever be not in the ark of
Noe will perish in the universal deluge. . . . I
know not Vitalis; I reject Miletius; I ignore
Paulinus.* Whosoever gathereth not with
thee, scattereth. . . . Who is not of Christ
is Antichrist." This father and doctor of the
Church, who merited special praise from St.
Augustin, could not have been ignorant of the
traditions of the Church or of the writings of
the principal fathers of preceding epochs. He
therefore speaks not only in his own name, but
as a witness of the opinion common in the
Church then and previously.

To his belief, thus clearly expressed, I add
that of St. Augustin, the great Bishop of Hip-
po, and the Doctor of Grace, the greatest intellect perhaps the Church in her long life has
possessed. In his defence of the doctrine on
grace he combated the heresy of Pelagius and
Celestius. He held councils against them, and
their heresy was condemned. The proceedings
of these councils were sent to Rome, to the
Pontiff, for approval. The approval was had

* The three contending bishops at Antioch.

from the Sovereign Pontiff Innocent I., and St. Augustin addresses in consequence these words to his opponents: "The acts of two councils have been sent to the Apostolic See; thence have come the rescripts (or answers); the case is decided; would that once for all error would cease!" We have here another witness of the tradition of the Church of undoubted capacity and credibility, the contemporary of St. Jerome, though his junior.

A short time later, in the year 451, we have the celebrated orator and Bishop of Ravenna and doctor of the Church, St. Peter Chrysologus, bearing witness to the same doctrine. He is writing to the heretic Eutyches, who, in opposing Nestorianism, which divided the personality of Christ, fell into the opposite heresy, that bore in consequence his name, and which confounded the two distinct natures of Christ. St. Peter replies to him in these very remarkable words: "The Magi, by their mystic gifts, confess Christ in his crib to be God, and priests with sad questioning discuss who it is was born of a virgin by the Holy Spirit. We exhort thee, honored brother, to attend obediently to what has been written by the most blessed Pope of the city of Rome; for blessed Peter, who lives and presides in his own chair, gives to those who seek it the truth of faith."

It is not necessary, dear brethren, that I detain you with further citations from the fathers of later date. These suffice, for they are of the first four centuries of Christianity, when apostolic tradition and practice were in the most flourishing state, even by the admission of those opposed to us, who readily admit that succeeding epochs are prolific in writers who bear witness to what they call the claims of Rome. Rather let us turn for a moment our attention to consider what was the action of the Church, whether she was consistent with these teachings of the fathers. This is very useful as a means of ascertaining the truth, as every moral body is apt to use its prerogatives to the full extent, and regulate its internal relations accordingly.

One very extraordinary course of action we see in the Church from the beginning, and one inexplicable, except on the supposition not only of the primacy of the Sovereign Pontiff, but also of his infallible teaching power, as inherent to that primacy : it is the appeal to the Pope in dogmatic cases. If the Pope were no more endowed with infallibility than the patriarchs of the Apostolic and Eastern Churches, how is it that he is the one appealed to and they are the ones that make the appeal? The fact of such appeal is beyond doubt. Even while the Apostle St. John was still living, St. Clement, successor of St. Peter, was the one to write to the Corinthians and settle their differences; not St. John. St. Polycarp, of whom I have said that he was St. John's disciple and Bishop of Smyrna, came to see Pope Anicetus to have settled the question of the proper day for the celebration of Easter. In the third century St. Denis of Alexandria was accused by the Christians of Pentapolis of the heresy afterwards taught by Arius. The accusation was made to Pope Dionysius, who called the patriarch to account and declared him innocent, the people acquiescing.* When we come to the fourth century, which saw the great Œcumenical Council of Nice, the second in number and the first after the Council of Jerusalem, we see a most remarkable instance of appeal. The Arians were all-powerful. They had deposed numbers of orthodox bishops from their sees. Among these were Paul, Bishop of Constantinople, and Athanasius, Bishop of Alexandria. To whom did they turn for redress? To the Bishop of Rome. Bear in mind, dear

* Vincenzi, *De Sacra Monarchia.*

brethren, that there was in question the divinity of the Word. But it was not only the great Patriarch of Alexandria who appealed to the Pope ; the Arians themselves, * notwithstanding they had the Emperor Constantius on their side, appealed also to the Pope. They asked him to call a general council ; but before he did so, taking due information of the bishops of various countries whom he called to his counsels, the Sovereign Pontiff condemned the Arians as deserters of the faith of the Council of Nice

It will be useful to cite another important appeal † of the fifth century, in which those appealing were the two most important bishops and patriarchs of the Church. One of these was St. Cyril, Patriarch of Alexandria ; the other was Nestorius, Patriarch of Constantinople, who was the author of the Nestorian heresy. St. Cyril opposed him ; but he, instead of yielding to the arguments of his learned and pious colleague, used such unjustifiable means, and showed such obstinacy in holding his false teaching, that St. Cyril referred the whole matter to Pope St. Celestin. Nestorius did the same, and the Pope, in consequence, pronounced judgment condemning the doctrines

* Alzog, vol. i. p. 381.   † Ibid., vol. i. § 119.

of Nestorius. I should detain you, dear brethren, too long were I to go through the facts of this nature, the prescriptions also of formulas of faith by such Popes as St. Leo the Great, Hormisdas, and Agatho, or even dwell on the instances in which the Sovereign Pontiffs gave evidence of their belief that they were the infallible guardians of the deposit of faith, by speaking to the assembled bishops, in even general councils, as their teachers, while the bishops, on their part, gave proof of their belief in such a prerogative of the successor of St. Peter, not only by their docile acceptance, but by their exclamations: "Peter has spoken through Leo,—through Agatho." This much will suffice to show how well grounded was the action of the tenth general council, which met at Lyons under the pontificate of Gregory X. (ann. 1274), who convoked it; and how consonant with truth was the conduct of the Greek emperor, Michael Palæologus, who had desired the council to be called, that the union of the two Churches, the Latin and the Greek, might be brought about. Here especially it was necessary that clearness of doctrine should be taught, and only the essentials of doctrine should be insisted on. What was done there? The great point to be settled was the primacy and

the resulting prerogatives of the Bishop of Rome.
As a basis of settlement the emperor presented
his profession of faith. In this document, speaking in the third person, he says: "The Holy
Roman Church holds the supreme primacy and
princedom over the universal Church, which the
emperor truly and humbly recognizes it received,
with fulness of power, from the Lord Himself,
in Blessed Peter, Prince or Head of the Apostles,
whose successor the Roman Pontiff is. And as
it is bound, above others, to defend the faith, so,
if any questions regarding faith arise, they are
to be settled by its judgment." We have here
the particular, individual Church, presided over
by the successor of Peter, declared by the emperor unerring; such is the declaration of the
one who has succeeded to all the rights of those
who had to his day fostered the schism of the
East. The council took action on this profession of faith; but what they say is still more
explicit, for, in the definition of the procession
of the Holy Ghost from the Father and the Son,
they say this is the doctrine of the Roman
Church, "*the mother and teacher of all the faithful*," "fidelium omnium mater ac magistra." *
There can be no doubt, dear brethren, that in

* *Hist. Conc.*, Labbe-Cossart.

thus speaking both the emperor and the council meant it was the judgment of the Sovereign Pontiff which was to be obeyed, and that his judgment in matters of faith and morals, when deciding controversies for the universal Church, was infallible. How could they look upon the official teacher of one infallible Church—that is, upon the Church of the Roman See they had judged to be infallible—in any other light? That such was the opinion of theologians at this time may be seen from the writings of the greatest among them, St. Thomas Aquinas. He was on his way to take part in the proceedings of this general council when he fell sick and died. In his great work, known as the *Summa*, he teaches most explicitly the infallibility of the Sovereign Pontiff.* In the first question of the second volume of the second part he uses these words: "It belongs to the authority of the Sovereign Pontiff to give a new edition of the Creed, to compose the symbol of faith "—"ad auctoritatem Summi Pontificis pertinet nova editio symboli"—and he gives as a reason the indefectibility of the faith of Peter. In another place of the same book, in the vi. art. of the second question, St. Thomas writes thus: "The faith of the Church cannot

*2. 2æ. q. 1. art x. Resp.

fail, for the Lord said to Simon Peter, 'I have prayed for thee, that thy faith fail not.'" St. Thomas identifies the living Pope, the one for the time being occupying the chair of Peter, with Peter himself, and to him does he apply these words of Christ promising inerrancy of faith to the Prince of the Apostles.

From this it is evident what the Council of Florence meant when it declared, with a solemn, formal decree, that not only was the Pope Chief Pastor of the Church, but the Doctor of the universal flock. We see, then, dear brethren, that though the form of the definition, the explicitness, and the solemn promulgation in the Vatican Council are new, the doctrine itself is not new. On the contrary, we trace it back in unbroken tradition from our own day to that of the Apostles. What the Church has done is simply to put in practice the advice so well known, so often quoted, of St. Vincent of Lerins: that, when the faith is to be taught, care must be taken not to say what is novel or new, but to explain the old faith in a new way ; that is, in the manner called for by the circumstances of the day. This, and this only, has been the line of conduct followed by the Church. Thus again has she given a proof of that Spirit who dwells in her, bringing to her mind whatsoever her Lord and Master had said to her in His intercourse with her on earth.

The dispositions we should cherish towards her are, first, one of thankfulness; for no jot or tittle of revealed truth is without its important influence for good on our lives. This doctrine of Papal Infallibility has such an influence on us all. By it we see the Church more united than ever before. By it we have received a sure criterion, by means of which we may be able to judge of God's truth with less danger of being led astray, of being left in doubt through want of a general council or of the consent of the universal Church dispersed throughout the world. There is no danger of any "uncertain sound" being given; for, when the Pontiff teaches the whole Church, we know what to believe, what to do. The words of St. Ambrose, "*Ubi Petrus, ibi Ecclesia*," are truer, if possible, now, than when he wrote them. To be with the successor of Peter is to be with Christ; to be separated from him is to be with the enemies of God. Whosoever heeds his voice, he is one of the sheep of his flock, of whom Christ said: "My sheep hear my voice." With this feeling of thankfulness should be coupled a disposition of great docility to the voice of the Vicar of Christ. His official *ex-cathedrâ* utterances as teacher of the faithful everywhere, with respect to faith and morals, we are to look on as revealed truth. This every one who professes the faith of the One, Holy, Catholic, and Apostolic Church is bound to do. But this is not enough. We are to look up to the Bishop of Rome as our guide in everything that appertains to our spiritual life, just as we are to look to the Church of God for this purpose. We are to reverence and to obey the one and the other, knowing that both are guided in turn by the Holy Ghost, whose one great duty imposed on Him, and willingly, lovingly discharged, is to care for all the members of the fold, His own members, His own temples. Let us cherish the docility of children towards their father, in our relations with the Head of God's Church on earth. Let us not imitate those Catholics who, if you were to believe them, stand in a continual dread of the Pope and his counsellors; who put themselves, as it were, in a condition of perpetual self-defence against the Sovereign Pontiff, as if God's Providence were not lovingly watching over all that he does, drawing good even out of the errors which may occur in the administration of affairs or in temporal matters, the decisions regarding which depend on information received. Be assured that, in those things which do not pertain to the supreme "magisterium," the opportunities of knowledge possessed by the Sovereign Pontiff far exceed those possessed by the most intelligent men; and how often have these latter to confess the fact, with the evidence had here before their eyes! God's Providence watches over those who obey; and not only are they free from the apprehension of any aggressions on the part of the Sovereign Pontiff, but they enjoy a tranquil trust in God, and possess at the same time, even in spiritual matters, not of faith, the safest guide it is given us here below to have. May God give us all this docility of spirit and subjection to his Vicar!

Lecture VII.

ON last Sunday I promised I would speak to you, dear brethren, of the decree of the Vatican Council. To-day I come to fulfil that promise. That decree declared the Sovereign Pontiff infallible in his definitions of faith and morals, when teaching *ex cathedrâ*, as the phrase is. It will be useful to put the decree before your eye in its integrity. In the fourth session of the council, after giving summarily the grounds of their decision, the proofs of the existence of the belief in this teaching from the very beginning of the Church, the Sovereign Pontiff and the Fathers go on to give the dogmatic definition in these words: " Whilst, then, we remain firm in the tradition of the Christian faith, which has come down to us from the beginning, we teach in accordance with this holy council, to the glory of God, our Saviour, to the exaltation of the Catholic religion, and for the benefit of all Christian people, and declare it to be a doctrine revealed by God, that the Roman Pontiff, when he speaks from his chair of doctrine (*ex cathedrâ*)—that is to say, when he, in the exercise of his office as Pastor and Doctor of all Christians, by reason of his supreme apostolic power, defines a doctrine of faith or morals to be held by the universal Church, in virtue of the divine assistance promised him in St. Peter, he possesses that infallibility which the Divine Redeemer willed His Church to have in the definition of a doctrine respecting faith or morals; and that, therefore, such definitions of the Roman Pontiff are of themselves, and not only when they have received the consent of the Church, unalterable. Should, then, any one—which God forbid!—venture to contest this definition of ours, let him be anathema."

Now, dear brethren, I can fancy a person hearing this decree, which pronounces the Sovereign Pontiff infallible, asking the following questions:

1st. What was the need or opportuneness of such a definition; especially since it is known that practically the Church always held it?

2d. How far does this decree extend, and what is the precise meaning of it ?

3d. What reply is to be given to those who bring forward such potent objections to it, taken from history and based on facts ?

To each one of these questions I propose to give a brief answer ; and I crave your indulgence if, in so doing, I may enter into some historical detail, necessary, however, to a clear understanding of the matter.

And, first, with respect to the need and opportuneness of the decree. Bear in mind, dear brethren, who the Sovereign Pontiff is and what are his prerogatives. He is the Supreme Ruler in the Church, and the one appointed by God, in the person of St. Peter, with full power to feed and govern the flock by teaching and commanding ; so defined the Council of Florence. To decide whether a decree confirming so strongly this power was needed, we must enquire whether any impediment had been put in the way of the full, complete, beneficial exercise of such power. A brief examination of historic facts will show us that such impediments really did exist to prevent the full and beneficial exercise of this authority.

The first assertion of the principles which afterwards became known as Gallican, from the country in which they had their origin and their greatest development, was during the period of the great schism of the West, when three claimants of the Papacy stood opposed to each other, one of these being the legitimate Pope, the others pretenders. Earnest men on all sides were busy in devising means to put an end to the divisions of Christendom. Among these was the learned Chancellor of Paris, Pierre d'Ailly. He put forth his doctrine regarding the power of the Bishops, teaching that they could, in extraordinary cases, sit in judgment on the Pope and depose him; which they certainly could not do, if the Pope is endowed with such power as the Vatican Council declares him to have. D'Ailly's distinguished pupil, the Chancellor Gerson, proposed this same doctrine at a critical period of the Council of Constance. The Emperor Sigismund, with the consent of John XXIII. and of Gregory XII., caused the council, which had been summoned by the bull of John XXIII.,* to meet at Constance, to settle the question of the papal succession. One Pope, Angelo Corrario, whose name will ever remain in

---

* John XXIII. convoked the council to meet at Constance, from Lodi by a bull of December 9, 1413.

honor, for he was the one whom history records as having the right to his position, but resigned it voluntarily for the sake of the Church, refused to come to the council, but sent his procurator, in his name, to resign, as agreed on with those of the opposite party, provided the other contestants did the same. The other contending Pope, Baldassarre Cossa,* unable to overcome his ambition, fled from the council. It was during this time, in which the council remained without a head, that the bishops voted the celebrated Canons of Constance,† which caused so much mischief in the Church, but which were never approved by Rome; for Martin V.'s approval extended only to what had been done "conciliariter" ‡—that is, "in council." That only can be properly so called, which is done when the assembly of Bishops has the legitimate Pope at its head, presiding personally or by his legates, and approving the decrees. These canons declared the superiority of the Bishops assembled over the Pope. What had contributed not a

---

* Cossa fled March 21, 1415, and was deposed May 29, 1415.   Corrario resigned July 4, 1415, unconditionally.

† Sess. iv., March 30, 1415. Sess. v., April 6, 1415.

‡ By the council as such—that is, the bishops in union with the Pope; presiding personally or by legate.

little to foster and increase Gallican ideas was the powers granted by Pope Urban VI. to the kings of France, on account of the danger of the people being led astray by the rival papal letters so freely circulated,—powers which permitted them to examine all pontifical documents before they were promulgated. This was a practical matter ; but, taken with the ideas then beginning to be broached, fashioned the opinions of ecclesiastics and statesmen in a manner unfavorable to the superiority of the Pope as teacher and ruler. The Canons of Constance began immediately to show their effect. Only a few years afterwards, at the general council called at Basle, the bishops of France especially, with a large number of clergy of the second order, rose up against the Pope, deposed him, and elected in his stead Amadeus of Savoy, under the title of Felix V. Amadeus, however, as soon as he was convinced of his error, resigned, * peace was restored, and the General Council of Florence gave the fullest definition of the power of the Roman Pontiff which had yet been proclaimed. You may readily imagine, dear brethren, that all this commotion could not take place without effect of some kind unfavorable to the Church.

* An. 1439.

Those who were hurt at the definition of Florence made use of interpretation to diminish its effect, and seized on the concluding clause of the definition, which referred to the doctrine "as contained in the decrees of œcumenical councils and in the canons of the Church." This phrase, they said, justified them in their opposition to the claims of Rome. They acknowledged the superiority of the œcumenical council, and a certain primacy of the Sovereign Pontiff; but not in the sense claimed for the Pope by what they called the Court of Rome, the Curia Romana, whose doctrines they stigmatized as from beyond the mountains which separate France from Italy, or ultramontane, in contradistinction to their own views, which they styled Gallican liberties and Gallican doctrine. From that day to this no general council convened by the Pope was ever in a condition to take up and decide this question among Catholics, so much was the Church occupied in combating the attacks of the sects which arose in the sixteenth century. The Popes, however, never neglected censuring those who taught the Gallican doctrines, as teaching erroneously ; but, inasmuch as the Gallicans always looked to a general council for a supreme decision, and the Sovereign Pontiff, as was natural,

he being the party concerned, did not put forth a
dogmatic decree on the subject, these doctrines
remained lurking in the Church, from time to
time showing themselves with. more or less
prominence, and with greater or less vitality.*
Governments, too, saw in Gallican teachings
what favored them against that which they
styled the encroachments of Rome, and, for
this reason, they patronized these doctrines
with all their might. The last century, and
the present too, witnessed this. The laws of
the Emperor Joseph, the new Church movement in Germany, the measures of Pombal in
Portugal, the doctrines of Giannone in Naples,
and the hostile articles surreptitiously appended to the Concordat of Napoleon I., whose
ideas were inherited by his nephew, and shared
by other crowned heads, all show this. What,
dear brethren, was the result? It was, as you
can clearly see, to hinder the full, complete,
and beneficial exercise of the supreme teach-

* This we see in the case of the Jansenist heresy, and in the declaration
of the Port-Royalist, Arnauld, that the consent of the universal Church,
necessary, as the Gallicans pretended, to an article of faith, had not been
given, if *one bishop* withheld his consent. But individual bishops are not
infallible. The error of one man, according to this assumption, could
thus hamper the whole Church; and it, moreover, could never be positive-
ly known whether the assent of each individual bishop had been given.

ing and ruling power of the Sovereign Pontiff. Whatever the Pope did was subjected to the most distrustful scrutiny, and reduced to its least expression, where it was not absolutely set at naught. Was this the spirit God wished should exist in His Church? Was this the docility to the voice of the Holy Spirit, working in the members of the Church to make them heed the voice of the Chief Pastor of their souls? Did Jesus Christ name Peter His Vicar, and transmit His power to his successors, that they might be looked on with distrust, and treated as enemies of the flock they were placed over? Dear brethren, we should certainly regard such obedience to the authorities of our respective countries as most undutiful, to say nothing further; and we surely cannot say less when we think of who and what the Sovereign Pontiff is. The beneficial influence of the Papacy in protecting the minds of the faithful from insidious error, in these days of universal diffusion of sceptical and anti-Christian ideas, called for a more untrammelled exercise of the teaching power of the Pope, and for the consequent removal of every impediment to that exercise. The first and greatest of such impediments was the doctrine known as Gallican; and not only was it natural, dear brethren, that the first œcumenical council after that of Trent should take the matter in hand and define the truth of the *ultramontane* doctrine, but it was the duty of the Fathers to do so. And we must be thankful to a merciful Providence that has restored confidence between the Pastor and his sheep, the Father and his children. The effect, dear brethren, has been most salutary in the Church. The peace and union within it are most consoling. The Bishops are more closely united with their Head, the Vicar of Christ, and Catholics with their Bishops. All this is of good omen for the future. The Catholic Church will present a more undivided front to the world, and it will only depend on the correspondence of individual Catholics, with grace of God, to exalt her in the face of mankind, and lead into the fold the multitudes that are without.

I come now to the meaning of the decree itself, in answer to the second question. But, before explaining what it means, it will be useful to explain briefly what it does not mean. So much has been said in the press and magazine literature on the subject that false ideas exist, not only among non-Catholics, but even among some Catholics. The first thing necessary to be remarked is, that the decree which declares the Pope infallible does *not* declare him *impeccable.* These are two distinct things. Infallibility may be said to belong to the intellectual order, impeccability to the moral order. I illustrate with an example : You will find persons who are truthful, who would not for the world tell a lie, and yet these very persons do not lead good lives ; they are dissipated or neglectful of their duties. Just so might it be with a Pope. There is no special guarantee he may not sin ; but there is a guarantee that he will always, in the circumstances mentioned in the decree, tell the truth about the faith—teach infallibly.

Again, the decree does not mean that the Pope will, under all circumstances, teach infallibly, but only when he is defining officially, *ex cathedrâ*, a doctrine of faith or morals to be held by the universal Church. All the assertions, dear brethren, you have heard about the Pope being infallible with regard to what does not concern faith or morality, are mere wild declamation, without foundation, and not worthy of thought.

The decree, however, does mean that, in the province of faith and morals, teaching what is to be held by the universal Church, the Pope cannot err, and that his definitions of this kind are infallible of themselves, and not by reason of the consent of the Church. In order to understand this exactly, we must bear in mind what the decree says.

It says, 1st: Tradition is that on which the Sovereign Pontiff takes his stand.

2d. That the council agrees with him.

3d. That the Pope is infallible by the assistance of the Holy Ghost, when teaching *ex cathedrâ* any doctrine of faith or morals to be held by the universal Church.

4th. That the consent of the Church is not needed to give force and inerrancy to such decree.

The Sovereign Pontiff and the bishops declare they adhere to tradition. I have already shown you, dear brethren, what the tradition is regarding the infallibility of the Pope. Tradition and Scripture, the written and the spoken word of God, are the source, and the only source, whence doctrine of faith and morals is to be drawn. The original deposit of the day of Pentecost was perfect, not to be taken from or added to. The anathema pronounced by St. John against any one who should add to or take from that deposit, the original revelation; the warning given by St. Paul lest any one be-

lieve those evangelizing other than he did,
stand to-day as in the days of the Apostles.
The Sovereign Pontiff cannot, the whole Church
with the Pontiff at its head cannot, alter one
iota of that deposit left with us by the Holy
Spirit. It follows, then, that when the Sovereign Pontiff wishes to define a doctrine of the.
Church, he must take his stand on what is
handed down by the Church, and find such doctrine in that tradition, whether by word of
mouth or by writing, in the written and spoken
word of God. It is true, dear brethren, that
the Sovereign Pontiff, being the judge of controversy in the Church, must be the one to decide when there is question of what is or is not
the tradition of the Church. This is his prerogative and duty. We who are gifted with
the faith have a certainty, surpassing human
knowledge, that in this he cannot err. The prudence and solicitude with which this power has
been exercised, especially in the decrees of the
Immaculate Conception and those of the Vatican Council, will convince all unprejudiced readers of the accounts which regard both that no
greater human precaution could be used. It is
true these dogmatical decrees may sound new
to unpractised ears. But they are only the old

doctrine in a new garb, developed in a new form, conclusions from the dogmas already defined; just, for example, as the dogma of the two wills in our Saviour was a new expression, a conclusion of new form, flowing from the dogma of the two distinct natures in Christ, the divine and the human; and, in defining such a conclusion of new form of expression, the Sovereign Pontiff and the Church are aided by the Holy Ghost. You understand, therefore, dear brethren, that this power of the Sovereign Pontiff is by no means an unlimited power. It is limited by the very nature of the case, as I have explained it. It is limited to doctrine of faith and morals, and to doctrine of faith and morals contained in the deposit of revelation and handed down to us. It may be said, too, in another sense, to be limited; that is to say, the Sovereign Pontiff will not and cannot act capriciously, even in such definitions, because he is under the guidance of the Holy Spirit, so that he will define only what the Holy Spirit, in His divine prudence, wills should be defined for the good of the Church. We can therefore rest assured that not only will there be no innovation in doctrine, but that whatever is decreed as of faith by the Pope will be that which the best interests of

the Church demand. It may clash, dear brethren, with the ideas and interests of this world;
but why should that trouble us? The ways of
this world are not the ways of God. If Jesus
Christ had waited for the consent or tolerance of
the world, He never would have preached His
doctrine. Moreover, every human being owes
obedience to God and His representative on
earth. We have no rights independent of God,
and all our self-assertion, when He or His representative, with due authority, speaks and commands, comes from a bad source, from ignorance,
or, what is worse, from a spirit of pride and rebellion against our Sovereign Lord and Master.
Hence it is, dear brethren, that it is our bounden
duty to give our most docile submission to the
Vicar of Christ, to accept his decrees not only
with external reverence, but with the internal
sacrifice of self, of our opinions, of our predilec-
tions in every respect.

It is useful here, dear brethren, to call your
attention to a point nowadays very often treated
of by the public press of Germany, France, and
of our own respective countries. The Sovereign
Pontiff, in his government of the Church, must
rely a great deal on the assistance of others.
For this reason he calls around him his cardi-

nals, his prelates, and learned advisers of the se-
cular and regular clergy known as consultors.
He forms these into various bodies, giving to
each body charge of some special department of
ecclesiastical business. It would be very difficult, if not impossible, to find anywhere such
competent and learned bodies of men. To their
ability and learning are to be added the prudence and care used in the treatment of business. These bodies are known as the Roman
Congregations. Now I come to what I wished
to say. The infallibility of the Sovereign Pontiff is limited to himself, and is exercised by
him alone. But the decrees of these Congregations are submitted to him, and must be approved by him, and, in consequence, you will find
appended to such decrees the phrase; "Ex audientia Sanctissimi"—"At an audience with our
Most Holy Father." What force is to be attributed to them from this? Are such decrees of
the Index, Holy Office, of the Congregation of
the Council, or that of Rites, especially concerned in matters more or less dogmatic, to be
looked on as infallible or as merely disciplinary?
This is the question so often asked, and on which
depends the solution of not a few objections
made against the Church. The answer is a sim-

ple one. The decrees of these Congregations are purely disciplinary. The Sovereign Pontiff has never any intention of deciding, through such instrumentality, dogmatic questions. He uses these bodies for the welfare of the faithful, as he uses those who act in his name elsewhere. The phrase, "ex audientia Sanctissimi," is nothing more than a formula of approbation to assure the faithful that such work is not done independently of the Sovereign Pontiff. But there is not the slightest intention of infallible teaching. Still, these decrees are to be most faithfully and docilely obeyed. For, not only is the Sovereign Pontiff infallible; he is also Supreme Ruler, with the authority from God given him in St. Peter. We are bound under grievous sin to obey him in grave matters, in a greater degree than we are bound to obey other authority, ecclesiastical or civil. The command of St. Paul, in the twelfth chapter to the Hebrews: "Obey your prelates and be subject to them," is especially applicable in this case. Conscience, therefore, dictates perfect submission to our superiors in all that is not sinful; and, therefore, as we do not expect infallibility in the ordinary commands of a superior, ecclesiastical or civil, neither are we to wait till we find it in the disciplinary decrees of the Roman Congregations before yielding to them a hearty obedience. What will be of use to make us more zealous in such obedience is this: that not all certainty is supernatural. There is metaphysical certainty, moral certainty, and physical certainty, and, in practical matters, a grade of probability approaching so nearly to certainty as to be styled moral certainty. Any one of these may be attained without transcending natural powers, without special aid of the Holy Spirit. Such certainty is, then, at the command of the learned and virtuous men who compose the Roman Congregations, and they are much more likely to have it, if we consider the universal, cosmopolitan character, if I may be allowed such an expression, of these bodies, and the means at their disposal.

The remaining point of the definition which is to be examined regards the declaration that the consent of the Church is not needed for the fixedness or inerrancy of the *ex-cathedrâ* decisions of the Sovereign Pontiff. The Sovereign Pontiff is the teacher of the universal Church. To the teacher must be subject those taught; it is incongruous that the disciple should confirm the master. Those who are taught are the Church, as we find the decree of Florence says. Certainly, the Church is in no danger of going astray ; but the same Holy Spirit who is working in its members to make them hold the faith, is working in the Sovereign Pontiff to make him teach it infallibly, and in the Bishops also to make them co-judges with him, and fit witnesses of the traditions of their individual churches, though their judgment is not necessary to give force to his. To express the matter in a few words, we may be allowed to say that the action of the Holy Spirit, though one, has a double effect : an active effect in the Sovereign Pontiff, a passive effect in the Bishops, who must teach as he teaches, and in the faithful dispersed throughout the world.

It was to be expected, dear brethren, that, when such a doctrine should be defined, the world would rise up in arms. The world and the prince of this world felt the blow as a mortal one, and we must not wonder at the resentment which followed, or at the wiles the enemy of man's salvation may employ. We often hear some well-meaning people deplore the definition. Why ? For two reasons especially : because they are too much attached to this world, its opinions, its comforts, to the friendship of people that they depend on ; or because they think harm has been done to the Church, and many souls have been kept out of the Church by this doctrine. Dear brethren, let us quicken our faith and look at the eternal years, the life to come; the spiritual life here, the eternal life begun here below, as Jesus Christ expresses it. What are all earthly gains or advantages in comparison with this? "He that loveth father and mother more than me is not worthy of me." We should dismiss the thought of inconvenience caused us as unworthy of us; whilst, on the other hand, we should consider that a valuable thing cannot be had without paying a high price for it. There could certainly be nothing more valuable than what secured to the Church of Jesus Christ the full, complete, and beneficial exercise of the teaching power of His Vicar, bestowed by her Divine Founder as a protection for weak, erring human intellect; consequently, we should really look on it as cheaply bought at the price of the petty annoyances it may cause us.

As for those who think souls have been kept out of the Church by this doctrine, there is room to question their view. Certainly many souls have come into the Church in consequence of it. Coming into the Church is the effect of grace, which may be resisted, as we know. But we may fairly ask whether those who say they are repelled by this dogma would have come into the fold. That there were others who left the Church on account of the dogma, I grant; but the history of not a few of these, as made known to us by the public press and one's own casual information, must lead us to suspect that other causes than the definition of the Council of the Vatican had long been at work to bring about a denial of the faith.

Before closing, dear brethren, I feel it incumbent on me to say a word regarding some very strongly-urged objections made against the infallibility.

They are of two kinds—they are theological and practical. The theological are based on historic facts, and, when strongly put, have a specious appearance which will undoubtedly move those who do not believe to look on the Church as having contradicted herself; while they may painfully impress those who believe, but have not examined the questions. With regard to such objections it will suffice to say, first, in general, that they have all long since been carefully and critically examined, and that they were again thoroughly sifted at the Vatican Council; and the result was that no case of erring in the official or *ex-cathedrâ* definitions of the Popes was ever found to be proven; secondly, that the case of Pope Honorius, which, in preference to the others found less tenable by the opponents of the definition, was particularly examined, and the difficulties, very serious at first sight, were satisfactorily cleared up. It is well to dwell for a moment on this case, as it is so often thrown in the face of Catholics. Pope Honorius wrote to Sergius, Patriarch of Constantinople, the author, in great part, of the monothelite heresy, seconding his views regarding silence on the subject of one or two wills in Christ. This is the ground of accusation against him. There are two opinions, each supported by able writers: that Honorius never wrote the letters at all, and this may be true; but, practically, we should take the second view, that he did write them. What follows from this second view? That Pope Honorius was condemned by the Sixth General Council because he did not define, not because he taught error. Such a condemnation is even an argument to show the belief of those days that the Pope ought to have defined, because he was the one divinely constituted to do so. Instead of defining, he wrote, if he be the author of the

letters, to Sergius, agreeing to impose silence on
the two parties, which had each, respectively,
as a watchword, "one will" and "two wills";
while, in these same letters, he teaches the very
doctrine of the two natures in Christ, each with
its proper "*energia*" (ἐνέργεια), or will, and he
excludes any conflict pertaining to the nature of
fallen man, that is, the law of the mind and the
law of the members, of which St. Paul speaks as
warring with each other in us. The Pope, Leo
II., who approved the council—and, dear brethren, you are aware that a council is valid only
in the sense in which it is approved by the
Pope—Pope Leo approved the condemnation of
Honorius, not as having taught heresy, but as
having neglected to do his duty.* And, as this
condemnation is the ground of all the others
which followed, it results that whatever terms
were used, heretic or other, nothing further than
this negligence, this "economy of silence," was

* The words of Pope Leo II. are: "Necnon et Honorium qui hanc
Apostolicam Ecclesiam non Apostolicæ Traditionis doctrina lustravit, sed
profana proditione immaculatam fidem subvertere conatus est" (Labbe
and Cossart, tom. vi. p. 1117). In the margin they have "immaculatam
maculari permisit," which is the exact translation of the Greek text:
"μιανθῆναι τὸ ἄσπιλον παρεχώρησε." Terms of condemnation
apart from the definition of doctrine are not infallible, because they regard facts learned by information which may or may not be correct.
There is much that is cloudy in the charge against Honorius. How
cunning and clamorous the Greeks were is well known.

meant. On the other hand, when we take into
consideration the fact of the hostility of the
Eastern bishops against Rome, which culmi-
nated in the Greek schism under Photius, and
later under Michael Cærularius, and the fact also
that the successors of Honorius, especially Pope
Hormisdas in his official formula of fidelity prescribed for the Eastern bishops, and Pope Agatho in the letters to the Seventh General Council, both solemnly declare that the Holy See of
Rome never taught error, we can readily acquit
the only Pope—that is, Honorius, against whom
an apparent case could be urged, of any erroneous teaching.

The other objections, I said, were practical.
They regard the effects of the decree with respect to governments. It is pretended that the
state of the Church has been changed, that new
rights have been asserted which interfere with
the rights of civil rulers. Both charges are
false. The state of the Church has not been
changed. The infallibility of the Pope has always practically been acknowledged ; the change
has been to destroy the errors of Gallican teaching. But the Pope will not encroach on civil
governments any farther than he ever did, if we
are to style encroachment the assertion of the

immutable, eternal principles of morality taught by the religion of Jesus Christ. He will teach nothing more than what has been taught before. The two orders, the ecclesiastical and the civil, are distinct in their object and sphere. Each must go out of its way to interfere with the other, and history has recorded far oftener the aggressiveness of the state than that of the Church, if it can be proved that the Church ever was aggressive. For, dear brethren, it is the style to speak of the Church as aggressive when she contends for the untrammelled exercise of the power God has given her, or for the possession of what she has justly acquired by the gratitude or piety of the faithful. Her Divine Founder placed her in our midst to correct us and to teach us, and she but imitates Him. As He was hated and persecuted, as He was reviled as a seducer of the people, a teacher of blasphemous doctrine, a plotter against the public weal, so must His Church and those who belong to it fare. She must conduct herself with the patience of which Christ gave her a sublime example. She has seen all those who raised their hand against her disappear. She is seeing them one by one disappear even now. Events are too recent to need explanation, and it may be that the near future has similar events in store to instruct mankind. Certainly, when we raise our eyes to that majestic palace which crowns the Vatican Hill, and think of the wonderful and venerable Pontiff whom duty and honor, even more than physical necessity, keep a prisoner there, it is impossible that in his preservation to this moment, which partakes of the nature of a prodigy, we should not see the hand of God preparing events which will redound to the good of His Church and of the world. Whatever may be, our duty is clear. We are to cling to the Vicar of Jesus Christ, our Infallible Teacher, whom God's angel protects, who is directed by the Holy Spirit in his beneficent rule ; we are to cherish towards him that docility of spirit for which the wise Solomon prayed, and which is a gift of the Holy Ghost. Adhering to him, God's representative here below, we adhere to God ; and God will reward us for our fidelity by an increase of faith, and by an increase of charity which will make us all be one with the Vicar of Christ and with each other ; which will make us, too, labor unceasingly by word and by example to bring those into the fold who know not the joy, and peace, and holy assurance which are the portion of those who call themselves children of the Vicar of Christ ; a joy, a peace, and

a holy assurance which are a presage of the
eternal happiness of those who will more really
one day be the children of our Father who is in
heaven, who is Truth itself, in whom our minds
and hearts will find perfect rest.

LECTURE VIII.

THE LITURGY OF THE CHURCH AND CATHOLIC DEVOTIONS.

"The priests and the Levites shall enter into my sanctuary, to come near unto me, and to minister unto me, and keep my ceremonies."—EZECHIEL xliv. 16.

IF we examine never so little into the various systems of religious worship which have obtained in the world, from the remotest ages up to the present time, we discover, dear brethren, that each one of them has had special outward ways of expressing its belief and of honoring the Deity. You find this truth as clearly illustrated amid the savage hordes of Polynesia, the roaming tribes of America, and the degraded types of Central Africa, as among the intellectual races of India and the cultivated pagan peoples of Greece and Rome, whose mythology and symbolism are the object of the study of the learned and the delight of the artist. It was reserved for professors of Christianity to attempt the complete exclusion of external forms in the worship of God. We hear continually from such Christians that true religion is spiritual; that God is not to be adored in "temples made with hands"; that forms bind down and hamper the free development of the soul; that "true religion and undefiled is to visit the widow and the fatherless," and does not consist in the observance of prescribed rites. Nevertheless, they have been only able, as I say, to attempt the exclusion of ceremonies in sacred things; for they have utterly failed in their main purpose. The reason is evident: they have done violence to nature, and it was impossible that they should succeed. The words of the old Latin poet are as true, and therefore as popular, now, as on the day when they were penned:

"Naturam expellas furcâ, tamen usque recurret"*

You may cast out nature even with violence, but she will come back. The universality of external forms in religion proves how natural they are. There may be errors in systems, but, be these what they may, it is a dictate of

* Horace, i. lib. ep. x. v. 21.

our nature to manifest our convictions outward-
ly. The reason is that the body is made for
the soul, and they form together a *compositum
humanum*—a composite human unity—under
the rule of one common personality. Soul and
body in man cannot act separately. Each is
continually influencing, or being influenced by,
the other. Moreover, man was made for society ; and those social relations for which the
Creator intended him require the exact correspondence of the body with the mind. Society is founded on truthfulness and fair-dealing. Words must mean what they say ; actions
must correspond with the internal state of the
mind. Such is the law of nature ; it is thus
that God has made man. Hence it follows
irresistibly that, in spite of all opposition, even
to the violent casting out of nature of which
the poet speaks, nature will still vindicate its
rights ; and truthfulness and fair-dealing, the
faithful correspondence of the actions of the
body with the state of the mind and soul, will
reassert themselves as the only solid basis of
social life.

We apply this principle, which cannot possibly be gainsaid, to religion. Mankind is convinced that there is a God ; that, in some way or

other, He has revealed His will to be worshipped by His creatures. This is a fixed foundation of man's belief. He is acted on by it during every moment of his existence. In danger
and in trouble he invokes and propitiates the Su·
preme Being as well as he knows how, and thus,
according to the expression of Tertullian, gives
the testimony of a mind naturally Christian.
The one special mode of honoring God—sacrifice—which we see used in the very beginning
of history, among pagan nations as well as under the Jewish dispensation, and continued by
Christianity, if we except the sects which lay
claim to the name of Christian, has always been
accompanied by forms of external worship.
The idea of the necessity of propitiating God
by sacrifice is, in fact, the pivot upon which
each respective system of religious worship
turns. Entertaining it, with whatever other
tenets, man could no more abstain from its external manifestation than he could repress his
nature. What was the line of conduct pursued
by the pseudo-reformers of the religion of
Christ? In proportion to their abhorrence of
any given dogma was the fury with which they
aimed their blows against its outward recognition—putting the axe, as it were, to the very

root, in order to do away with whatever necessarily kept alive in the souls of the faithful the truths they denied. The doctrines they for a while retained were of course accompanied by some corresponding rite or observance; but, as faith gradually dwindled down to its lowest degree of meagreness, forms of worship assumed a commensurately sterile aspect, which is mistaken by those who still cling to this last shred of religion for the simplicity of the Gospel. The basis upon which they found their alleged convictions will not, however, sustain a moment's serious scrutiny. God Himself, in the Old Law, ordained that certain ceremonies and rites should be established. He bade Moses observe and make what He had commanded, according to the pattern He had shown him on the Mount, and each of the manifold, nay, almost numberless, requirements of the levitical and sacrificial law was prescribed with a minuteness of detail which affords overwhelming evidence of the will of the Almighty concerning the manner in which His chosen people were to appear in His presence. Christ came to fulfil the law of Moses; but that law, together with its attendant ceremonies, having been one of types, became unnecessary when the great Antitype appeared of which they were only the figures. Indeed, the continuance of their use would have signified a disbelief in the reality of the possession of what they prefigured. The Apostles and teachers of the early Church were compelled to discountenance and condemn this very abuse, which grew up in the first century after Christ among Judaizing Christians. But, besides what was mainly typical in the Ancient Law, there were a multitude of signs of veneration of God, and of ways of adoring Him, which, under whatever form of worship, would either naturally suggest themselves to the human mind, or might fittingly serve for that purpose. Jesus Christ Himself made use of some of these. We read that our Lord prayed aloud ; that He prayed on His knees ; that He sang a hymn with His Apostles ; that He instituted the Blessed Eucharist and the Sacrifice of the Christian Altar, bidding His disciples " do this in remembrance of " Him. Moreover, we behold Him washing the feet of the disciples, touching with spittle taken from His divine mouth the ears of the deaf person ; we see him mixing spittle with the clay which He applied to the eyes of the blind man, restoring him thereby to sight—all typical acts, intended to prefigure the intrinsic power of His holy sacraments, in which matter, by the efficacy of His omnipotent word, was to become endowed with virtue to cause life and grace in the soul, as water in Baptism, chrism in Confirmation, and oil in the Sacrament of Extreme Unction. It was during His forty days' life on earth after His Resurrection that our Lord organized His Church, and gave the last instructions regarding the sacraments. When we are desirous of knowing what commands were given, what the institutions and ceremonials were with which our Divine Saviour vouchsafed to enrich His Church during the period which preceded His ascension into heaven, we turn our eyes to the traditions it has handed down from the beginning, and, applying the rule given by St. Augustine and by St. Vincent of Lerins, believe that what has always been held everywhere, and by all Christians, is most certainly not error, but the truth which was received from Jesus Christ by His Apostles. We adhere to the forms thus transmitted from one generation to another, and deem it unlawful to alter them in the least. Subsidiary forms may be introduced or modified by the Church ; but those derived from the Apostles, implying dogmatic teaching, are unchangeable.

Here occurs the question, Who may make changes of any kind? Who, in the past, has been empowered to do so, or may do so now?

It is obvious, dear brethren, that, as the forms of religious worship hold the closest relation to belief, the power of regulating them can belong to none other than the highest teaching authority. The danger of erring would be too great were the right left to individuals, or even to individual churches, of introducing or modifying ritualistic observances. The sentiment expressed by Pope Celestin I., in his letter to the bishops of Gaul, underlies the action of the Church in this matter. He tells them that the law of prayer is to determine the law of belief--"Lex orandi statuat legem credendi." These two laws are so intimately blended together that they cannot be disjoined in ecclesiastical legislation ; and it is for this reason that the Supreme Authority of the Church reserves to itself the power of deciding all questions relating to divine worship, and permits no forms or ceremonies which it does not sanction. It is strange that a principle so natural should be for an instant a subject of cavil. We find it adopted by the ancient Romans, whose *pontifex maximus* was exclusively vested with the prerogative of regulating worship, and the same has been ever the case with most other pagan religions. It is only in our day that we witness individuals arrogating to themselves the functions of liturgical legislators. How is this novelty to be explained? Are they actuated only by a morbid spirit of innovation, or do those who are called Ritualists not rather recognize inherent defects in their own church which they are conscientiously striving to remedy? I believe, if I may be allowed to express an individual opinion on such a subject, that in at least the vast majority of cases the latter reason is the correct one. The investigations which followed the Tractarian movement of over thirty years ago have led many to the discovery that the so-called Reformation was unworthy of the name, and that even those who flattered themselves they were weeding out tares had, in reality, plucked up the good growth of sound doctrine instead, destroying with it its foliage of outward forms. Now that the Ritualists have attained to a belief in certain doctrines hitherto repudiated by Anglicans, it is but natural, in accordance with the principle I have laid down, that they should seek for their expression in the rites adapted for that purpose.

So far, dear brethren, there is nothing of which
we may not respect the motive ; but their action
in undertaking to regulate their liturgical forms
themselves is manifestly unsafe, and even, if
many details known to most of us are considered, indefensible.   Were their course only
one of contradiction to their own church, such
as it is, there would be no ground for condemnation ; but experience has shown that what began in conscientious opposition has, in too many
instances, developed into an assumption · by individual ministers of a practical infallibility,
and retain those dependent on them in a
spiritual bondage unjustifiable in the eyes of
God and anti-Christian in spirit.   They do not
seem to bestir themselves, as tenderness of conscience would suggest, to examine the claims
of the Church which they know has never ceased to hold the doctrines and to employ the
corresponding forms which have gained their
slow consent ; but, presuming upon their position, no matter how much they may differ
among themselves in opinion, they prevent those
guided by their counsels from either consulting
with Catholic priests, reading Catholic books,
or frequenting Catholic places of worship.
While these gentlemen boldly assert their

right of private judgment against their own bishops, they absolutely refuse the same right to those they spiritually preside over. It is no reply to recriminate against the Holy Catholic Church of Rome the charge we bring against them. It is not true, as they pretend, that the Roman Catholic priest exercises a similar jurisdiction over his flock. There is no parity in the case. No Catholic priest, as you are aware, dear brethren, is at liberty to follow his own private judgment. He has over him a supreme authority to direct him, to which he is bound implicitly to submit to. Those over whom he rules are careful to ascertain well that he is in communion with, and his teaching is sanctioned and approved of by, that authority. This test of their priests' rectitude and orthodoxy is ever before the eyes of the people, and saves them from the possibility of being misled. The simplest uneducated Catholic occupies, dear brethren, a safer position, has a more sublime confidence in his faith, than the most enlightened non-Catholic can possibly possess. His motive of assent to the teachings of faith is identical with that of the most learned theologian—the presence of the Holy Spirit teaching in the Church and preserving it from error. The answer given to her master or mistress by the poor servant-maid when asked why she believes some doctrine, "Because the Church teaches it," is often listened to with a pitying or contemptuous smile; but it is the great philosophical and theological reply found in the sublime pages of a St. Augustine or a St. Thomas of Aquin. The illiterate Catholic knows that his priest is in communion with his bishop, and his bishop with the Pope, the Vicar of Jesus Christ on earth; and this is his guarantee that the anointed servant of God to whom he goes to confession, or whom he consults, will not mislead him. But what assurance could he have if his priest had no superior, no one to whom he was bound to be united in faith, but taught by his own unaided reason, and dictated liturgical observances from his own ideas of the æsthetic? The answer is obvious; but such is the incomprehensible position in which those are placed who follow the Ritualistic movement, instead of logically coming into the Church which they know holds the very tenets they are striving for.*

* What certainly justifies the Ritualistic movement in England and elsewhere, and makes out an unanswerable case against the Anglican prelates, is the discovery of the frescoes in the Church of St. Clement at Rome. Among others, there is one representing St. Clement saying Mass.

In addition to the safeguards just mentioned, there are, dear brethren, others of a special character to prevent the Catholic from being misled. However protected from danger of going astray the priest or the bishop may be, the Church does not allow either the one or the other to lay down laws respecting the liturgy. That most important function is reserved for a committee, or, as it is commonly styled, a congregation, whose duty it is to watch over everything regarding divine worship. It is known as the Congregation of Rites. It is composed of twenty-four of the most distinguished members of the Apostolic College of Cardinals, one of whom acts as president or prefect. Besides these, there belong to it

This painting is in the subterranean church, and is considered to be of the ninth century, if not earlier. At that time the artist was firmly persuaded that St. Clement wore the vestments now in use in the Catholic Church; and if he was so convinced it is a sign that the use of such vestments was traditional in the Roman Church in his day; they held possession by prescriptive right. Looking at this picture, you see the altar with its canopy and hanging-lamp; upon the altar the chalice and the paten; near them the open missal, and in it you read familiar Latin words of the Catholic ritual: " Dominus vobiscum " and " Pax Domini sit semper vobiscum." St. Clement stands at the altar, with the vestments of a Catholic priest, the colobium or chasuble, the pallium, or it may be the stole, after the manner of the Greeks, and the maniple. His attendants carry crosses, incense, and tapers. In a fresco of the transfer of the remains of St. Clement, at this same church, all the processional ritual of the Church is most exactly represented. How could honest non-Catholics, educated in prejudice against our liturgical forms, fail to be impressed by the sight of all this ? It was perfectly natural they should be.

nine prelates and twenty-five consultors, all men of note for their learning or special ability. Any matter of importance is first studied by the consultors, then by the cardinals and their special assistants, and the vote of this congregation of these twenty-four cardinals, subject to the approval of the Sovereign Pontiff, is what decides the question. It is thus clear from the very nature of the case that the precautions against mistake are rendered effectual, and that a disciplinary decree issued, with the sanction of the Pope, by such a body of men precludes, as far as human means render it possible, any liability to even the smallest error. How safe such a rule is for Catholics is manifest. What a contrast between this and the solitary, though earnest, minister, who is the *de facto* infallible teacher of his congregation !

It is under the guardianship of the high controlling authority of the Congregation of Rites that are placed those forms of worship which show themselves from time to time in, as it were, a new character, which startle non-Catholics and cause them to exclaim that the Church has changed and has introduced new teachings. I refer to what are generally known under the name of "devotions." By devotions in general, dear brethren, are meant those forms of worship whereby we express not only our belief, but also some special affection of our heart which we cherish towards God, or towards any object either directly or indirectly connected with God or referring to Him. We are carefully to distinguish in every devotion two things—the motive and the object. This is very important, in order that misunderstanding may be avoided. The motive is God, or relation to God in any way; the object is manifold, according to the nature of the devotion, being the material object around which the devotion centres. There is still another distinction to be made. As every devotion has for its object, directly or indirectly, some person, it is necessary to bear in mind that there is a triple worship sanctioned by the Church. A proper understanding of this will make manifest how falsely the Church is sometimes accused of idolatry. The first degree of worship is what is known as *latreia*, from the Greek word signifying divine worship, and is paid to God alone; the second is *hyperdulia*, a compound Greek word, the components being *hyper*, above, and *dulia*, the worship or homage paid to a servant—a servant of God. This second degree of reverence is paid only to the Mother of God. The third and last degree is known as *dulia*, and is the worship or honor paid to a servant—a servant of God—a saint.

Let us consider for a moment this devotion to the saints, to illustrate what I have been saying, especially as it is so much objected to by those who are not Catholics. I must state, at the outset, that this tenet of the existence of communion between the saints in heaven and the faithful on earth is an apostolic tradition which we find embodied in the Apostles' Creed. We believe that we can pray to the saints; that they pray for us; that we are helped by their prayers and by their merits in God's sight. In the Catholic doctrine the saints in heaven, the faithful on earth, and the souls in purgatory form one body in the sight of God, who views their good actions and merits as one, and permits each to share in the merit of the others; prayer being the chief means by which that merit is applied to individuals. There are not wanting instances and proofs from Holy Writ to substantiate this teaching. The first evidence we may take from the example and prayer of Lot. Almighty God stayed His vengeance on Sodom and Gomorrah at the prayer of Lot, and had only ten individuals been found whose actions were pleasing in His sight, these cities would not have been destroyed. In like manner we read in the Book of Job that the Almighty told those who had upbraided Job in his afflictions, and with whom He was therefore angry, that He would not listen to them, but that they were to ask Job to pray for them, —"Orabit pro vobis servus meus Job."

In the fifteenth chapter of the prophet Jeremias, first verse, we read : "And the Lord said to me : If Moses and Samuel shall stand before me, my soul is not towards this people." Again, in the fourteenth chapter of Ezechiel, twentieth verse : "And Noe, and Daniel, and Job be in the midst thereof ; they shall deliver neither son nor daughter"; that is to say, God would not listen to their pleadings in behalf of their people. And how often are we assured of the benefits granted by the Almighty for his servants "Abraham, Isaac, and Jacob's sake" !

In the New Testament we find St. Paul * begging the brethren to pray for him : "I beseech you, brethren, that you help me in your prayers for me to God"; and St. James declares that "the prayer of the just man availeth much."

* Ad Rom. xv.

In commenting upon the text of St. Paul, Cardinal Bellarmine argues as follows: "If it was lawful to ask the brethren then for their prayers, and it was no derogation from the intercession of Christ to do so, it cannot be derogatory to the merits and intercession of Christ to pray to the saints in heaven," for the saints have the same merits they had on earth. Their merit has remained the same because it was secured to them by a good death; while, on the other hand, they are now no longer in a state to merit further. Moreover, the saints have greater charity for us and are more inclined to pray for us than when on earth. Again, the saints are aware that we invoke their aid, because of their knowing everything in God, and they rejoice, as Christ declares the angels do, "over every sinner that repenteth." The objection made against the devotion to the saints, that it is not commanded in Holy Scripture, has no force, because we see the angels appealed to by holy men in the Old Testament, as recounted in the books of Daniel, and Tobias, and even of Genesis. Jacob speaks of the angel who always aided him, and prays him to bless his children. These, dear brethren, are but a very few of the instances to be found, in

Scripture, of prayer addressed to spirits, and of the aid rendered by them to man. And when to these positive words of the Holy Bible are added the experience of ages, the apostolic traditions, such wonderful and incontrovertible effects of the invocation of saints as the miracles related by St. Augustine, and the wonders which may be daily witnessed, at the present time, at Lourdes and elsewhere, it is impossible for a mind free from prejudice to gainsay this devotion.

Now I return from this digression to apply what I have said to the worship of saints. I spoke of the distinction between the motive and the object in all devotion. The motive we have in venerating the saints is to honor God in His friends, in those He deigns to honor. The saints are the friends of God. All the excellence they possess they have received from Him ; and, therefore, in honoring such excellence or virtue, we are honoring God. We revere self-denial, the sacrifice of one's life in a good cause, as for one's country, even when we behold such hero-ism in a pagan. The three hundred of Ther-mopylæ have received a just meed of praise in every age. But this is mere human veneration. It does not extend beyond the individual himself, and its effects cease there, excepting in so far as the example may incite us to noble deeds. But the case is far different with the saints. We honor their sublime virtue, but refer the honor to God. It is God who is adored in them, and therefore our reverence is a religious act which not only encourages us to follow the standard of holiness held up to our admiration, but also obtains for us the blessing of the Creator, the assistance of His saints, and the help of the Holy Ghost to lead a supernatural life. This motive, therefore, is one which directly refers or appertains to God and the religious life.

The object of the devotion itself is the human being whom we honor, or those things which belong to or relate to him ; such as relics or images. Around these the acts of our devotion centre, and in venerating or employing them in any pious way we always have for a motive the homage due to God in His servant. Through that servant we hope to obtain the graces we stand in need of. We do not, therefore, transfer from God to them anything that belongs to Him, still less do we derogate from the intercession of Jesus Christ ; but just as God bade those suing for pardon go to Job, and St. Paul besought others to pray for him, without derogating from our

Lord's intercession in any way; so we, with equal propriety, implore the saints to intercede for us, and honor the pictures and relics which remind us of them, in order that we may ob- tain what we ask for.

Again, I made the distinction of the three grades of worship—*latreia, hyperdulia,* and *dulia;* that is, the worship of God, of the Blessed Virgin Mary, and the inferior veneration paid to the servants of God. In this devotion to the saints the first grade of worship, *latreia,* or divine worship, is excluded; the other two only obtain, the *hyperdulia* for the Mother of God and the *dulia* for the saints. It is clear from this, dear brethren, as you perceive, that no such thing as worship in the sense in which non-Catholics use the word is chargeable against the Church in its reverence of saints; so much so that lately, in the judgment rendered in the Folkestone case,* Lord Penzance clearly stated no one would ac- cuse Catholics of paying the worship that be- longed to God to saints and their images. An inferior honor only, and that, inasmuch as they are friends of God, is given to them; and we have seen that this practice is founded on tradi- tion and Scripture, and has been sanctioned by

* Risdale Case.

innumerable miracles testifying the approval of Almighty God.

What I have said, dear brethren, with regard to the devotion to the saints may be applied to all the devotions of the Church. In the devotion to the Most Sacred Heart of Jesus the motive is the divinity or the Divine Person of Christ, the object His material Heart, the symbol and organ of His love, united to that person, ruled by it, and one with it, just as our heart or our hand is one with us, is ourself. Whatever homage is paid to the object is paid to the person. So, too, with regard to the devotion to the Most Precious Blood of our Saviour. These devotions, once recognized and approved by the Sacred Congregation of Rites, are lawful and useful, and merit our veneration. The supervision of these devotions by the Sacred Congregation is our unfailing safeguard against the possibility of going astray.

I can imagine, dear brethren, some one objecting that such forms of religious worship appeal to the feelings, while true religion ought to be calm and intellectual, and in no way based upon excitement, because this latter has the effect of obscuring the mind and preventing it from clearly understanding and discerning between what is reasonable and what is unreasonable. The answer is a very simple one. First, we are protected from mistakes by the supreme direction of the liturgical legislation in the Church. If, individually, any one err, the means are within his reach of instantly correcting his error. Secondly, those who would exclude feeling from religion make a grave mistake. God is our Sovereign Master, and must be honored with our whole being, and not with a part of it only. Moreover, God is love; He is the supreme good; and because He loves us He is to be loved in return; and we are bound to love Him for Himself, because He is this Supreme Infinite Good. All the affections of our nature should, therefore, be given to Him. The fact that the Catholic religion accords with nature in directing our affections towards God by its devotions is a proof that it comes from Him who is the Author of nature; while it also explains the strong hold it has on all classes of those who profess it. The omission to take into account the yearnings of the heart is, in great part, the cause of the decreasing hold of Protestantism upon the masses; while it is an evidence that it comes not from the Author of nature. So great

is the want the masses of our people experience in this respect, that they are seen going
after sensational forms of religion, to the
absolute exclusion of dogma. This explains
the excitement caused lately by the revivals in
England and in America, which have simply
astounded the cultured clergymen of non-Catholic communities. It also explains why the
denomination known as Wesleyans or Metho-
dists have gained so largely in proportion as
other sects have declined. "Nature cannot be
cast out; she will come back." The divine
wisdom of the Founder of the Christian Church
provided for the requirements of human nature;
but, to guard against every danger of error, laid
down clearly the rules by which His followers
should be guided. The security we enjoy is
an additional title to our gratitude, and should
be a reason to make us correspond with the
spirit of the Catholic Church. In all the Church
does she has our interests at heart. It was by
her liturgy that she taught pagan and barba-
rous nations respect and love for authority, and
for all that pertains to divine worship. It was
and is her veneration for the inspired Word of
God which has caused the Scripture to be looked
up to with such universal reverence. We are

told by Tarasius, Patriarch of Constantinople, who took such a prominent part in the Seventh Œcumenical Council, in his letter to Pope Hadrian I., that the Gospel was placed on the throne in the midst of the council; and in the Vatican Council the Bible was put upon the altar in the midst of the fathers, and honored as the word of God speaking to them. These examples we ought to profit by. We should strive to enter into the spirit of the various festivals and devotions of the Church. It is by this means that we shall be enabled to educate our souls in the real life—that of the spirit—and to separate ourselves from that baneful materialistic life which prevails at the present day. Thus, too, all the aspirations of our nature will be corresponded to and satisfied; incipient yearnings will be implanted within our souls to be realized hereafter. Those yearnings and tendencies, satisfied as far as possible here below, will be more and more purified and strengthened, until they shall find in a happy eternity the only object which can content them—Infinite Truth and Infinite Good, the reward of all those who hearken to the words of God's Church, placed by Him as a guide to our feet and a light to our eyes in this vale of darkness.

LECTURE IX.

PENANCE.

OUR Lord and Saviour Jesus Christ, dear brethren, came upon this earth to redeem us, to atone for our sins, to wash them away with His precious blood. " Christus oblatus est semel ad multorum exhaurienda peccata," says St. Paul, Hebr. ix. 28—" Christ was offered once to exhaust the sins of many." That one expiatory act of our Redeemer's, as far as its efficacy is concerned, blotted out every sin committed from the beginning of the world to the end of time. But with regard to the positive effects of the Redemption, there is a contingency ever to be borne in mind by the sinner. St. Augustine teaches us : " He who created you without your concurrence, will not save you without your concurrence." It stands to reason, dear brethren, that no prince or ruler can forgive a rebellious subject, if that subject persevere in his rebellion, or continue to foster a seditious spirit. Hence it follows that, although Christ died for all, not all will be saved ; because it is a fact of daily, nay, of hourly, experience that men not only live in a state of open revolt against God, of wilful sin ; not only manifest no desire to repent, but even glory in their guilt and determinedly die in their iniquity. We continually witness examples of this fact, even in this centre of the Christian world, where the means of salvation are, as it were, thrust and obtruded upon us by divine mercy with such lavish prodigality. This is the first reason why the merits of Jesus Christ, of themselves all-sufficient, are often inefficacious in their result.

There is another cause, however, why they remain without effect. It is because the declared will of God has conditioned the application of those merits upon certain actions, the use of certain means, without which no one, ordinarily speaking, can profit by the infinite graces obtained for mankind by His Son. I have said ordinarily, because the hand of Almighty God is not shortened, and, in His inscrutable mercy, He may vouchsafe to have recourse to extraordinary ways ; but with these we have nothing to do. It is the most supreme folly to look to extraordinary means of salvation, to the exclusion of the use of the ordinary means ordained by God. Therefore, in what I am going to say, dear brethren, I shall speak only of the ordinary means left by God in His Church for our justification. Unless these are properly employed by man, the merits of Christ will avail him nothing ; and it is, consequently, of the most vital importance for each one of us to know precisely what they are.

The means, dear brethren, whereby the merits of the Passion and Death of our Lord Jesus Christ may be applied to us, are the holy Sacraments of the Catholic Church. A sacrament is a sacred outward sign, instituted by Jesus Christ, to signify and impart grace to the soul. Jesus Christ, the author of nature and of grace, took matter and added to it, by His word, grace and spiritual efficacy, just as He did with the clay which, mingled with spittle from His sacred mouth, He put upon the eyes of the blind man to restore him to sight. He instituted, as the Catholic Church teaches, seven of these sacraments, three of which, from their imparting spiritual life where it did not previously exist, are generally denominated sacraments of the dead ;

that is, of those dead spiritually. These are Baptism, Penance, and Extreme Unction. The first our Lord has declared to be absolutely necessary to the life of the soul: "Unless you be born again of water and the Holy Ghost, you shall not enter into the kingdom of heaven." The second and third restore lost grace. To-day I wish to speak to you of the second; that is, of the Sacrament of Penance—a sacrament which Christ instituted, taking for its material basis the form of a judicial proceeding, including both the criminal and his judge, and adding thereto His divine grace. Such is the nature of the Sacrament of Penance, the means provided by God for receiving anew spiritual life which has been lost after Baptism. This sacrament, named by the Fathers of the Church a second baptism, a painful re-entrance into life, a plank of safety after shipwreck, is, as you know, dear brethren, scouted as an invention of later days, and an innovation, useless, to say the least, if not absolutely wicked. I hope to make it evident not only that this view is an utterly false one, but that, 1st, this sacrament has its type in the Old Law; 2d, that it was instituted by Christ, and is obligatory upon all; and, 3d, that the power of forgiveness in the Church, thus bestowed by our Lord, is unrestricted with respect to sin and its spiritual effects.

The confession of one's sins in detail is not, dear brethren, a practice which has no later date than the advent of Christ. We read in the Old Testament of sacrifices offered for particular sins ; as, for example, the ram for a sin of negligence, and the goat for a sin of ignorance.* Naturally, the offering of such sacrifice was a confession of sin. But this was not all. We are told, in the fifth chapter of Leviticus (v. 4 et seq.): If any one swear and keep not his oath, "let him do penance for his sin, and offer of the flocks an ewe, lamb, or she-goat," or other sacrifice, if unable to offer one of these, "and the priest shall pray for him and for his sin, . . . and it shall be forgiven him." Now, according to the opinion of learned Hebrew scholars, the phrase in the original text, which St. Jerome in the Vulgate has translated, "let him do penance," signifies, literally: "*Let him confess himself of what he has done sinfully*"—that is, the culpable person was required to make an external, oral manifestation of his transgression.† The word *confiteor* is frequently

* Numbers v. 6–8; ib. xv. 24.
† The Hebrew text, Lev. v. 5, has, וְהִתְוַדָּה אֲשֶׁר חָטָא עָלֶיהָ as

found in the Bible, and is to be interpreted, according to the context, in various ways, as is also the case in English. It is made use of in celebrating the divine praises. The precision of Scripture, in enumerating the minutest circumstances, renders it still more evident that the sin it describes was to be orally confessed, and not left to be supposed. Moreover, the confession was a secret one. The offering for secret sin was prescribed, to be partaken of by the priests only, and not by members of their families, and no portion was allowed to be taken out of the temple. This custom is attested by the Jewish historian Josephus, who says: "Whoever sins, and his conscience alone knows it, and has no one who can reprove him, will offer a ram according to the law, and the priests, on the same day, will eat the flesh of it in like manner in the temple."

This is not all. There is nothing more useful, in order correctly to understand the Old Testament, than to study the usages of the Jews

above—"Let him confess himself [with regard to] what he has done sinfully." The verb from which the word וְהִתְוַדָּה comes is יָרָה or רָדָה, —jecit, manu indicavit. The reflex form here used means *manifest himself,* confess. Here this word is determined in its meaning by what follows, אֲשֶׁר חָטָא עָלֶיהָ—"*What he has done sinfully.*" (See Vicenzi, *La Confessione Vocale,* Rome, 1850.)

themselves.   Now, the most celebrated rabbins expressly inculcate in their writings that "when Israelites sacrifice for voluntary or involuntary sin, if they do not repent and make a clear and well-stated confession of their sins, their sacrifices will be of no avail."   And the Jew Philo, writing on Victims,* confirms what I have just quoted from Scripture, that "no part of the victim offered for sin was to be taken out of the temple, for the sole reason, *that his sins might not be cast up to the penitent.*"   "These sins," he observes, "must be reserved to the sacred precincts in which the expiation is made." So explicit are the testimonies on this point of confession in detail, that we are enabled by them more fully to comprehend the words of St. Matthew, chapter third, when he relates that "Jerusalem, and all Judea, and all the country about Jordan went out . . . to John the Baptist, . . . confessing their sins."   The necessity of confession was, it is plain, universally recognized at the time our Lord commenced His preaching.   The final dispersion of the Jews, the loss of their priesthood, and the confusion of their tribes rendered it impossible for them to maintain the sacrificial precepts of the Mo-

---

* *De Victimis,* ed. Coloniæ Allobrogum, an. 1613, p. 653 E.

saic law. But, nevertheless, they strove, and still strive, to cling as closely as circumstances allow to its observances, and they have substituted for confession to a priest either the accusation of themselves before those whom they have set apart to act in the priest's stead, or, in some secret place of their abode, before God alone.

You are well aware, dear brethren, that the Old Law was one of types, destined to have their realization in the New Dispensation. The sacred rites of *the* Jews were beneficial, in consequence of *the* disposition and prayers of those who performed them. Of themselves they did not bestow grace. The sacred rites of the New Law work grace of themselves, though, of course, requiring the consent and desire to receive them well on the part of the recipient. They produce sanctification *ex opere operato*, according to theological language, *by the work done;* while the Jewish rites produced grace *ex opere operantis*—by the act, that is, of the individual receiving or fulfilling them. Jesus Christ raised this practice of the Jews of confessing their sins before their priests to the dignity of a sacrament, instituting a tribunal wherein the priest should sit as a judge in His name ; hear and pass sentence on the self-accuser; pardon the offences committed, if contritely acknowledged, and impose satisfaction in proportion to the degree and nature of the guilt. The act of our Lord in establishing priestly jurisdiction over sinners is narrated in the Sacred Text. In the Gospel of St. Matthew * He foreshadows the institution of the Sacrament of Penance when He tells His Apostles: "He who will not hear the Church, let him be to you as the heathen and the publican. Amen, I say to you, whatsoever you shall bind upon earth shall be bound also in heaven; and whatsoever you shall loose upon earth shall be loosed also in heaven." The fulfilment of this solemn promise of Jesus Christ we witness in scenes which occurred after His resurrection. We read, in the twentieth chapter of St. John, that, on the day He rose from the dead, Christ stood in the midst of His disciples, and said to them: "Peace be to you. As the Father hath sent me, I send you." Observe the wording of the mandate. Our Lord had already said: "All power has been given me in heaven and on earth." He had wrought a miracle to prove His power to forgive sins; for, when He healed the paralytic man, He had pronounced the words in the pres-

* Matt. xviii. 18.

ence of the Jews: "Have courage; thy sins are forgiven thee." The Pharisees and Scribes, you remember, murmured at this, saying: "How can this man forgive sins?"—only God can do that. Jesus, who knew their thoughts, replied to them: "Why do you murmur? Which is easier to say, Thy sins are forgiven thee; or, Take up thy bed and walk? But that you may know the Son of Man hath power to forgive sin, turning to the paralytic man, He said: Arise, take up thy bed, and walk." Now, our Lord, who had thus given proof of His omnipotence, again declares His power, and sends others with the same authority precisely that the Father had vested in Himself: "As the Father hath sent me, so I send you (verse 22), and, when he had said this, He breathed upon them, and He said to them: Receive ye the Holy Ghost: whose sins ye shall forgive, they are forgiven them; whose sins ye shall retain, they are retained." Here we see bestowed upon the Apostles and their successors this tremendous power of sitting in judgment as God, by the commission of God Himself, and with the promise that the sentence they pronounce will be ratified by Him. Our Lord is the God of *all:* "There is no other name under heaven whereby man can be saved."

"No one cometh to the Father," He declares,
" save through me," and I depute you to act in
my stead, "for as the Father has sent me, I
send you." All who come to me must come
through you, for we are one. Therefore, dear
brethren, this tribunal of penance is a tribunal
that does not admit of exemption from its jurisdiction. Even those who, by reason of perfect
contrition, are pardoned before confession, are
bound to present themselves to it. Its jurisdiction is, therefore, commensurate with that of
God Himself. A twofold power is imparted to
the Apostles and their successors : that of binding and that of loosing. The power of loosing
is exercised when the sentence of remission, of
absolution, is pronounced ; that of binding is
exercised when the minister of God refuses to
absolve ; and those who have sinned, and do not
approach to this tribunal, remain in the bonds
of sin. Unless they come to confess humbly
their sin, the minister of God will not pronounce
the sentence which will loose them from these
bonds ; and that refusal to loosen is ratified in
heaven, and they remain bound, their sins are
retained.

It follows from the nature of this tribunal,
dear brethren, as is evident from what I have

said, that all, without exception, who have attained the age of reason and have sinned, must present themselves before the priest of God, in the Sacrament of Penance, as a necessary condition for forgiveness of sin. It follows also, both from what I have said of the custom prevalent among the Jews, as well as from the Sacrament of Penance being a sacred tribunal, that a detailed confession of sin must be made. The priests of the Old Law had to distinguish between leprosy and leprosy, in physical cases; and this was a figure of the moral diseases of the soul which the priest of the New Law is to judge of. The Sacrament of Penance has, besides the immediate effect of remission, one of healing and protecting, and both these effects require detailed knowledge in the minister of God. A judge must, in fact, know the quality of the deed done, both in order to pronounce sentence as to whether or not it falls under the law, as well as in order to apply the remedy, impose the punishment, and exact satisfaction for the well-being of society. If a priest, in the tribunal of penance, have come to him one who has defrauded his neighbor, how is he to know what to tell him, or what restitution to exact of him, unless the particular sin be confessed ? And yet we know from the thirtieth chapter of the prophet Ezechiel that the amount stolen, or the pledge unjustly retained, must be given back, otherwise the sin is not remitted.

It was in such a sense that this power conferred by the words of Christ, and this duty imposed in consequence of it, were understood in the Church. From the earliest period of the Church such was her teaching, such her practice. St. Augustine speaks of this power; so also do St. Ambrose, St. John Chrysostom, St. Gregory Nazianzen. Ecclesiastical history is full of facts regarding the Sacrament of Penance. There was the private confession of sins to the priest; and there was the public confession of sin, to which was annexed a system of public penance. All works on ecclesiastical history, even the most elementary, treat of this. Sometimes the penance was undergone not only by public sinners, or by those who made public confession, but also by others voluntarily. The penance undergone varied with the character of the sin, both with respect to kind and duration—weeks, months, and even years of penance being assigned. Hence derives the familiar expression used in the Church, which so often scandalizes those who are not Catholics. They hear of so many days, or weeks, or years of indulgence, and do not understand that by such words is meant dispensation from these days, or weeks, or years of penance, by substitution of other work by the authority of the Church. In order, however, dear brethren, that we understand this thoroughly, it is needful that we dwell on the necessity of satisfaction for our sins, of penance for them, whence flows the doctrine of indulgences.

For confession, such as will justify in the sight of God, you are aware, dear brethren, that there are absolutely required contrition, hearty sorrow for sin, based on a supernatural motive ; confession in detail to a duly authorized priest ; satisfaction imposed by him ; and, finally, on the part of the priest, the sentence of absolution. Against this point of satisfaction those who deny the necessity of good works very naturally rise up. Such is the logical consequence of their system, and we must, therefore, not be surprised at this denial. That their teaching has not only no foundation, but contradicts the words of Scripture and the words of our Lord Jesus Christ, condemning to everlasting fire those not doing good works, we have already seen. Against this particular manifestation of their system, this denial of the necessity of satisfaction, I wish to present you some valid reasons based on Scripture itself.

In every grievous sin we are to distinguish, first, the guilt of sin; secondly, eternal death resulting from it; thirdly, temporal punishment incurred for it; and, fourthly, the necessity of reparation.

Of the guilt of sin and its eternal punishment Christ Himself tells us, where He speaks of certain heinous offences, and says, those "who do such things will not enter into the kingdom of heaven." It is not necessary, therefore, to delay on this point. By the sentence of absolution pronounced on a sinner, in due disposition to receive it worthily, the guilt and the eternal punishment are remitted. Not so is it with respect to the temporal punishment incurred, and the satisfaction necessary. These two remain to be undergone, and the proof is at hand. We have several remarkable instances in Scripture in which this fact is unmistakably shown.

The first among these I select is the case of Adam and Eve in the Garden of Paradise. They had sinned; but, on their repentance, God pardoned them. He, nevertheless, addressed them words of terrible import, even while promising the Redeemer, through whose merits their sin was forgiven. "Cursed is the earth in thy work. . . . In the sweat of thy face shalt thou eat bread until thou return to the earth, out of which thou wast taken: for dust thou art, and into dust shalt thou return."* Toil, suffering, disease, death—all these are so many penalties to be undergone by Adam and his posterity, notwithstanding his sin has been remitted.

Another instance we have from the life of the Royal Psalmist. King David had been guilty of murder and adultery. For one year he lay in his moral lethargy, heedless of the sad state of his soul. God had pity on him, and sent to him the prophet Nathan, who by a parable convinced him of his guilt. The words of the prophet, "Thou art the man," sounded to him as the upbraiding voice of an offended God, and he fell prostrate, crying: "I have sinned against the Lord." His repentance was sincere, and merited that the prophet should say to him: "The Lord has remitted thy sin." But he added: "Because thou hast made the enemies of God blaspheme, the child that is born to thee shall die." Here was a temporal

* Gen. iii.

punishment inflicted by God upon David, even after his sin had been forgiven. There are many instances, dear brethren, in Holy Writ, from which we can deduce the same truth, that, after sin pardoned, temporal punishment is still to be undergone. Almighty God must in some way be appeased, His justice satisfied, in this way, by punishment inflicted by Him. But not only does He require this; He demands also voluntary affliction of ourselves, penance done willingly or in obedience to the priest to whom we confess. This He accepts, and, in consequence, remits what we deserve to suffer. Of this, too, there are instances in Scripture.

The first of these is one that not only occurs in the Old Testament, but has the approbation of Jesus Christ Himself in the New. We are told in the book of Jonas that, at his prophesying the destruction of Ninive, the people, and even their king, did penance by fasting in sackcloth and ashes. They repented of their sin; they turned from their evil way; they confessed their offences; but they were not content with this. They thought they must satisfy the offended justice of God, not only by doing what natural justice dictated—restoring what had been ill-gotten, repairing the damage done to the reputation of others, forgiving injuries—but, besides this, they did penance, a penance full of self-affliction. They had sinned by self-indulgence ; they punished themselves by denying themselves what they naturally craved—food and comfort. If we were to believe the sects of to day, we should say that these were works of supererogation, entirely unnecessary, in fact perfectly useless. But, dear brethren, a greater than any of the prophets of to-day, a greater than the prophets of any day, approved that penance, full of fear and full of suffering. Jesus Christ tells us what the Ninivites did at the preaching of Jonas, and reprimands the Jews, because, though there was present before them One greater than Jonas, they did not imitate the penance of the Ninivites.

Again, we have the phrase " do penance " frequently occurring in the Sacred Text. The first preaching of our Lord, as we read in the fourth chapter of St. Matthew, was in those words.

What He meant by them is evident from the language He employs in praising the Ninivites. Again, when He tells us of the rich man who died and was buried in hell, He merely says that he did not give alms, but feasted splendidly every day, and was clothed in purple and fine linen, giving us to understand the necessity of self-denial and mortification to atone for our sins. So far, then, dear brethren, are we to be from regarding these works of penance as useless, according to the theory, of those out of the Church, that we must look on them as an integral part of the atonement for our sins demanded of us by God. This is, therefore, a part of the satisfaction we owe Him. To some extent the debt is discharged by confession, and by performing the penance imposed on us by the priest. But as, generally, yet more remains to be done by way of satisfaction, the Church comes to our assistance. Call to mind what I said a few moments ago. The power given the Church by Jesus Christ is unlimited. "All power has been given me," He said : "as the Father hath sent me, I send you. Whose sins ye shall forgive, they are forgiven them." Now, we know that sins are forgiven only through the merits of Jesus Christ. Those merits, however, are not confined to Him alone ; they embrace all that, by means of His coming on earth, He did in Himself or in others. I say in others, for all the good works of others are His work ;

without Him they would not and could not have been performed. The works, therefore, of Christ, and the good works of the faithful throughout the world, and in every epoch, are one vast treasure which belongs to Christ. In virtue of the doctrine of the communion of saints, we know that we share in each other's good works and merits. Now, this great treasure of merits which belongs to Jesus Christ He puts at the disposal of the Church, so that the Church can make use of it at will. How she does this I will explain presently. I call attention beforehand to the fact that it is a higher power, a more noble act, to restore grace to the *soul than to* remit the punishment of it. The change from the state of sin to a state of grace is one of the greatest of God's miracles, greater than raising the dead to life. It is not strange, therefore, that Christ, having given such wonderful power to His Church, should not have restricted her with regard to what was less, the remission of the temporal punishment due to sin, especially when we hear Him say: "All power has been given me in heaven and on earth: as the Father hath sent me, I send you." Armed, then, with this plenitude of power, with this treasure of the merits of Christ and of His saints at her disposal, what does the Church do? She applies, in virtue of her supreme power, these merits to the faithful, in lieu of their own satisfaction, under certain conditions, which, if fulfilled, procure for them a remission of the temporal punishment to be undergone after the sin has been remitted in the tribunal of penance. This is what is known as an indulgence. An indulgence, therefore, is not, as it is so often falsely charged, a permission to commit sin ; nor is it a pardon of sin ; but it is a remission of temporal punishment to be undergone after sin has been pardoned. You understand now, dear brethren, how it is that indulgences are spoken of as being of several days, of several years. This wording, strictly just, is taken from the early discipline of the Church, as I have observed before. When penance had to be done for days, and months, and years, what Christians gained by those periods of self-denial and punishment is bestowed by an indulgence, which, therefore, takes the same title of so many days or so many years. The practice of granting indulgences is coeval with the Church of the martyrs. On the same principle of vicarious atonement and satisfaction, of the communion of saints, the Church accepted the merits of martyrs while suffering, and at their written request would excuse from their penance those in whose favor the request was made. This is a fact of early history which cannot be called in question. In consequence of this same principle of the communion of saints, of the unity of the Church triumphant in heaven, the Church militant on earth, and . the Church suffering in purgatory, where those are detained who left this life without having discharged their debt of temporal suffering, the good works contained in this treasury of the Church are applicable *per modum suffragii ;* they are offered to God as a supplication for the remission of the punishment due to souls after death, which God may or may not accept. What one has gained for himself he may freely give for these souls, that, as we read in the Book of Machabees, they may be loosed from their sins.

Such, dear brethren, is the wonderful means the patient love of God has invented to rescue us from sin and from its direful effects. To us it is an ordinary thing; we have been used to it from our childhood, and it may happen that we do not appreciate it as we ought. If we could understand its full reality, our tongues

would call on the whole universe to thank God
for this great glory manifested in the remission
of sins. We should also have a higher idea of
the goodness of God; of that wonderful love of
which He gave us some faint view when He
represented Himself as the Good Shepherd, going after His one stray sheep, while He left the
ninety-nine; or when He speaks of Himself as
the Father receiving back to His bosom His
prodigal child. These are, after all, but faint
images of God's love towards us. Knowing
this, we should endeavor, with great faith and
confidence, to make use of this means of recon-
ciliation with Him. For one thing must be evident to every one: if God, on His part, has
done so much for us, it is surely not His intention to leave us to our own weakness in making use of this great sacrament, on the contrary
He will aid us always, where He finds the least
disposition in us to make a good and beneficial
use of it. The acts of faith, of humility, and of
sorrow we exercise in doing so bring with them
special graces; while the Sacrament itself bestows
actual graces, and assistance against the faults
we confess. No one, therefore, no matter how
steeped in sin, should draw back from this pledge
of God's mercy. Especially at the holy seasons

of the year, an acceptable time, a time of salvation, should all approach to this sacred tribunal, and share in those spiritual gifts, in comparison with which all the treasures of earth are
as dross

Lecture X.

I COME to speak to you to-day, dear brethren, of one of the great mysteries of our holy religion—a mystery wonderful, surpassing the utmost stretch of unaided human imagination or conception; a mystery so extraordinary as to seem almost proposed for the purpose of repelling men from accepting the religion which teaches it; a mystery which, at its very first announcement by the divine Founder of our faith, had precisely that very effect. This mystery is that of the Real Presence of the Word made Flesh, under the appearance of bread and wine, in the Sacrament of the Blessed Eucharist. In the announcement of no other mystery did our Lord show so evidently His appreciation of the difficulty of the acceptance of it by men, as in proposing for their belief the doctrine of the Real Presence. A moment's consideration of His manner of speaking in the sixth chapter of the Gospel of St. John will make this evident to the most ordinary capacity.

When Jesus Christ announced the doctrine of His divine nature, He appealed simply to facts which every one knew; that is, to the miracles He had wrought. When He spoke of the regeneration of man, He confined Himself to declaring the necessity of being born again of water and the Holy Ghost. He taught in the same way, when He unfolded the mystery of the Blessed Trinity and that of the redemption of the human race. "The works that I do, 'these bear witness of me." "If you do not believe me, believe the works that I do." Such was His reply to objections and to incredulity. The answer could not be gainsaid, and served as a ground of acceptance, in the case presented. But to this He now adds a special and most emphatic exhortation to faith in Him, expounding the difficulty of it, and pointing to the source whence alone it could come.

You remember, dear brethren, that the sixth chapter of the Gospel of St. John opens with the wonderful miracle of the multiplication of the five barley loaves and two fishes. Five thousand people were sated with this food, and twelve baskets were filled with the fragments that remained over and above from what had been eaten. The multitude were so struck with this astounding prodigy that they exclaimed: "This is of a truth the prophet that is to come into the world" (verse 14). In accordance with the ideas they had of the Messias, who, they thought, was to rescue Israel from bondage, they would have made Him king; but He fled away from them. They went seeking Him, and found Him on the other side of the sea which He had crossed miraculously the night before. He tells them that they seek Him, not because they had seen miracles, but because they had eaten of the loaves and were filled. He chides them for being so gross and material, and says to them: "Labor not for the meat that perisheth, but for that which endureth unto life everlasting, which the Son of Man will give you. For Him hath God the Father sealed" (verse 27). Here Christ begins His remarkable preface which inculcates the necessity and also the difficulty of faith. For those He speaks to ask Him: "What shall we do that we may work the works of God? Jesus answered them and said: This is the work of God, that you believe in Him whom He hath sent" (verses 28, 29). They immediately begin to contest, as it were, His claim to their belief, and refer to the miracle of the manna which Moses had given in the desert, as if showing that He had done nothing to surpass the miracle of Moses. Therefore they require a further display of His power. The only answer Christ returns them is this: that their fathers ate manna in the desert, but that manna was not bread from heaven; and He adds: "My Father giveth you the true bread from heaven. For the bread of God is that which cometh down from heaven, and giveth life to the world." When they said to Him: "Lord, give us always this bread," He answered: "I am the bread of life; he that cometh to me shall not hunger; and he that believeth in me shall never thirst" (verses 32–35). Our Lord, as is evident, speaks of spiritual hunger and spiritual thirst. The Jews did not misunderstand Him here; but they murmured against Him, because He had said He came down from heaven, for they say: We know His father and mother. It is here, dear brethren, that our Lord gives us clearly to understand the difficulty of faith, and how it is a gift of God, for He says: "Murmur not among yourselves. No man can come to me except the Father, who hath sent me, draw him." We shall see that Jesus reiterates this assertion, after having fully declared the doctrine of the Blessed Eucharist. In this present connection He prepares the ground, and makes this declaration that He may use it at the decisive moment of the complete manifestation of a doctrine which was to tax so seriously the faith in Him of all His followers. He is steadily leading the way up to this doctrine by inculcating the paramount importance of faith. If we weigh well this mode of proceeding of Christ, it is impossible, dear brethren, that the thought of some important doctrine to be revealed should not present itself to our thoughts. For never yet has He so spoken; never yet so rebutted the arguments of His opponents; never yet has He gone so directly against what they esteemed to be the teaching of the law. He is substituting Himself for it; vindicating for Himself exclusively the power to speak in the name of God, and putting Himself forward as the only means of salvation. He even excludes from that salvation all those whom the Father does not draw to Him; and, by His words expressly uttered here, He gives all to understand that belief in what He is going to say can only come from the Father. All this must certainly make us look forward to some weighty revelation, and that Christ hastens to declare. He repeats anew: "I am the bread of life. Your fathers did eat manna in the desert, and are dead. This is the bread that cometh down from heaven; that if any man eat of it, he may not die. I am the living bread that came down from heaven. If any man eat of this bread, he shall live for ever; and the bread that I will give is my flesh for the life of the world" (verses 48-52). The passage is here made from the spiritual sense of faith and grace as inculcated by the phrase, "I am the bread which came down from heaven," to what we may call the material or real sense of the flesh of Christ; not that this sense is excluded by the context in the prior portions of our Lord's discourse, for He had this in His mind as He spoke; but His primary motive was to prepare those present not only with respect to the absolute need of faith, but also with regard to the proper sense in which they were to understand the real eating of His flesh. All that has gone before, down to this fifty-second verse, is but a preface and preparation for the doctrine which Christ now unfolds to those present. The Jews who had been scandalized when Christ declared that He came down from heaven, are far more so now. At first they murmured; now they strive among themselves, and say: "How can this man give us His flesh to eat?" It is evident that they understood Christ in a carnal manner; but the words were so unusual, the circumstance so extraordinary, that one cannot be surprised that nature, unaided by grace, should not have understood them. Yet what does our Lord go on to say? Does He, as was frequently His wont, explain to them or to His disciples the hidden meaning of the words? His only answer is a most solemn asseveration, and a more explicit declaration of the doctrine: "Amen, amen, I say unto you, except you eat the flesh of the Son of man, and drink His blood, you shall not have life in you. He that eateth my flesh, and drinketh my blood, hath everlasting life: and I will raise him up at the last day." Could any one imagine, dear brethren, a more efficacious way of confirming those who had murmured and were scandalized, in their opinion that the Lord really did intend His flesh to be eaten, and His blood

to be drunk? How easily He might have
said: I am but speaking figuratively; I only
mean the partaking of what will be a representation of my flesh and of my blood separated by death. But He *does not* say anything of the kind; on the contrary, He con-
tinues even more explicitly: "My flesh is meat
indeed, and my blood is drink indeed. He that
eateth my flesh, and drinketh my blood, abideth in me, and I in him. As the living Father
hath sent me, and I live by the Father, so
he that eateth me, the same shall live by
me." There was no one present, dear brethren, who misunderstood Christ as regards the
fact. Those words were too explicit; they could
mean but one thing. The objection that the
wording here is a Syro-Chaldaic idiom, and figurative, cannot be admitted. That idiomatic
phrase refers to calumny and injury. It would
have been foolish to interpret Christ as making
calumny and abuse of Himself a condition of
eternal life. No one in His presence was absurd
enough to entertain such an idea for an instant.
All understood Him unmistakably as to the fact;
they mistook Him as to the way. They understood Him as opposing to the eating of the manna of the Old Testament a physical action of eat-

ing in the New Dispensation, and of participating
of tho very flesh, as they saw it, of Him who was
speaking to them.   His words confirm them lu
this idea, for they are explicit : "This is the
bread which came down from heaven."   You remember, dear brethren, that the Jews, quoting
the Scripture, had said : "He gave them bread
from heaven to eat."   Christ replied that Moses
did not give them bread from heaven, but that
the bread which came down from heaven gave
life to the world.   That manna of which He
again speaks, He says, did not give life ; for
"your fathers did eat manna in the desert, and
are dead."   Thus Christ confirms the Jews in
their interpretation of a physical eating of His
flesh.   The effect of this eating will, however, be
different; for "he that eateth this bread shall
live for ever."   The natural effect of these words
was immediately visible.   Before, it was the
Jews that strove among themselves, saying :
"How can this man give us His flesh to eat ?"
Now it is His disciples who begin to murmur,
and remark : "This saying is hard, and who can
hear it ?"   Here, dear brethren, it is of interest to
observe the manner in which our Lord acts with
the disciples, for it affords a strong indication of
His meaning.   When He related the parable of

the sower who went out to sow his seed, and His disciples asked Him what this parable might be, He replied: "To you it is given to know the mystery of the kingdom of God; but to the rest in parables, that seeing they may not see, and hearing they may not understand" (Luke viii. 10). And He explained the parable to them. Why did He not explain to these disciples this parable? Because, dear brethren, it was not a parable. He meant what He said. He meant that they were to eat His flesh and drink His blood. They who had been with Him so long; who had heard the words of grace which daily fell from His lips; who had witnessed the wonderful miracles He had wrought, ought to have understood that, however improbable it might seem to nature, still He was by His power able to devise a way by which what seemed gross and carnal would be avoided, and the truth of what He had uttered be nevertheless maintained. But, like so many who have come after them, they confided, even when God Himself was speaking to them, in their own reason, and they bore the consequence. Christ sees their danger, and calls their attention to His future ascension into heaven as a sign that would prove to them the truth of what He had said; and we may hope that when His ascension was afterwards beheld or heard of by them, it recalled them to a sense of the criminality of their unbelief. He saith to them: "Doth this scandalize you? If then you shall see the Son of Man ascend up where He was before?" (John vi. 63). He adds here words which have been the subject of dispute between the Catholic Church and the dissidents of the last three centuries and a half: "It is the Spirit that quickeneth; the flesh profiteth nothing. The words I have spoken to you are spirit and life." With regard to these words, it is obvious that our Lord pronounced them as a direct reply to the objection which had been made to His teaching. It is natural that His answer should correspond to the nature of the cavil of those who murmured; especially as there was no reason why He should speak for any other purpose. If we accept the objections of non-Catholics and their interpretations, the harmony of the entire context of this remarkable chapter is destroyed, and Jesus Christ is made to appear as having deliberately laid a snare for the weakness of those who had hitherto followed Him—a supposition irreconcilable with His unspeakable goodness and tenderness for their welfare. If, however, we receive His words as replying exactly to the objections of His disciples, solving their difficulty, while maintaining the doctrine of the Real Presence, and of the real participation, by eating, of His Body and Blood, everything becomes harmonious. It does not require much acumen, dear brethren, to understand that this is the safest rule of interpretation. When, therefore, our Lord says: "It is the Spirit that quickeneth; the flesh profiteth nothing," the meaning is that the eating of His flesh in a carnal manner is not what He intends; that they are not to eat it as they would meat, for in that way it would profit them nothing. For that which profiteth is the Spirit, which is with my flesh, my divinity, that gives value to my Body and my Blood. You are, therefore, to partake of my Flesh and of my Blood in a manner to derive from them the spiritual benefit which comes from the presence of My Divinity within you. You are to receive Me in such a way that My natures will not be destroyed or separated, and, therefore, in a mystical manner, which will nevertheless realize the words I have hitherto uttered: those "words are spirit and life,"—a Hebraism for spiritual and life-giving. Such, my dear brethren, is the obvious interpretation of the words of our Saviour. Such, too, is the explanation given to us of them by the lucid and penetrating intellect of St. Augustine.[*]

Our Lord, dear brethren, having, at this point, fully expounded His doctrine, recurs again, as though always having before His eyes the difficulty of the mystery, to the indispensability of faith from above, and repeats what He had said previously in the forty-fourth verse: "There are some of you that believe not. Therefore did I say to you that no man can come to me unless it be given him by my Father." We are informed by the Evangelist St. John (vi. 67) that "after this many of His disciples went back, and walked no more with Him." Is it at all probable, dear brethren, that this would have happened if our Lord had only spoken of a commemoration of His Passion and Death by bread and wine?

Let us pass to a brief consideration of the institution of the Blessed Eucharist, and examine whether our interpretation is borne out, or whether this idea of a commemoration by bread and wine is substantiated. We read in the twenty-sixth chapter of the Gospel of St. Matthew (verse 26), that our Lord, as St. Luke also

* Tr. xlvii. in Joannem.

relates, was at the Last Supper with His twelve Apostles, and, "whilst they were at supper, Jesus took bread, and blessed, and broke, and gave to His disciples ; and said : Take ye and eat ; this is my body. (verse 27:) And taking the chalice, He gave thanks.; and gave to them, saying : Drink ye all of this. (verse 28 :) For this is my blood of the New Testament, which shall be shed for many unto the remission of sins." Nothing can be more explicit than these few words of our Lord. He declares that what *but a moment* before was bread is now His Body ; *what* but a moment before was wine is now His Blood. We see the perfect realization here of what He had promised in the passage of St. John I have explained. The explaining away of the word *is*, as done by the followers of Calvin and Zwingle, if not by all Protestants, is a manifest violence done to the text. Whenever *is* is equivalent to "represents," or means "is figurative of," that meaning results from the nature of the matter spoken of, and from the context. But, in the present instance, the nature of the case clearly requires that the word *is* should be received in its natural and ordinary sense of being. For we have seen that Christ had spoken to His disciples of something that would try their faith,

and to such a degree that the power of the Father alone could make them accept His teaching.
What difficulty, however, would there have been
in accepting a nude commemoration by a supper in which bread and wine were partaken of ?
Such a thing was not beyond the sphere of reason ; indeed, required no further exercise of faith
whatsoever. Moreover, Christ had promised a
bread that would replace the manna. If the
Body and the Blood of Christ were not hidden
under this form of bread and wine, the antitype
would be of less value, be less extraordinary
than the type or figure. Who would be so ir-
reverent, dear brethren, as to assert that this is
possible ? It stands to reason that the words of
Christ are practical propositions, effecting what
they signify, and truly converting the bread into
His Body and the wine into His Blood. By
virtue of these words, under the species of bread
is only the Body of Christ ; under that of wine
only His Blood ; though, as you know, dear
brethren, as Christ dieth no more, His Body and
His Blood, and His soul and His divinity, are no
longer separable, and are there by concomitance
present under each species. This interpretation
of these words of consecration is borne out by
the constant tradition of the Church of God, the

infallible body in which dwells perpetually the Holy Spirit. I have no intention of detaining you, dear brethren, with numerous citations; but I cannot refrain from quoting the testimony, on this important subject, of two or three of the Fathers of the Church.

The first is a remarkable passage of the apostolic Father St. Ignatius of Antioch, who, writing against those who denied to Christ a real body, says, in his Epistle to the Christians of Smyrna: "They do not admit the Eucharistic offerings and oblations, because they do not confess that the Eucharist is the Flesh of our Lord and Saviour Jesus Christ."

St. Irenæus, who, you will remember, is a Father of the second century, in the second chapter of his fifth book against heresies, writes: "The chalice which is derived from a creature, He pronounced to be His own Blood; and the bread which is from a creature, He pronounced to be His own Body."

Tertullian, also a writer of the second century and early part of the third, in his book against Marcion (iv. n. 40) says: "He made the bread He had taken that very Body of His."

And St. Augustine, in his two hundred and twenty-seventh sermon, thus speaks: "That bread which you see on the altar, sanctified by the Word of God, is the Body of Christ; this chalice, rather what the chalice has in it, sanctified by the Word of God, is the Blood of Christ."

The time is too limited, dear brethren, to permit my dwelling longer on tradition with reference to this subject, or to develop the argument which proves the Blessed Eucharist to be a sacrifice as well as a sacrament. Both these themes would require a discourse for each. Rather permit me to present you with a fact which proves both the one and the other; and this you will more readily allow, as facts bear more weight with them than words. This fact is one of Christian symbolism.

In the Catacombs of St. Calixtus, on the Appian Way, there exists a group of remarkable frescoes. It consists of a centre-piece, and of two lateral illustrative pictures. These frescoes are pronounced, by the unanimous verdict of competent judges, to belong to the first half of the third century. The central picture represents a banquet. Seven persons are reclining at a table, as was the custom in ancient times. There are two fish upon the table, and before it are eight paniers of bread. The fish, in Christian art, is known to be a representation of Christ, or the

Christian. The acrostic Ἰχθυς, with which you are familiar, goes back to a very early date, and was used as the name of Christ; for the letters composing it are the initials of the five Greek words, signifying Jesus Christ, Son of God, Saviour. Tertullian uses it in his book on Baptism (c. i.): "Nos omnes pisciculi secundum Icthun nostrum Christum"—"We are all little fish, after the manner of our Icthus, Christ: we are born in the water, and only by remaining in the water are we safe." Optatus Milevitanus, a Father of the fourth century, in his comment on the book of Tobias, also speaks of the fish as a type of Christ. He says that the fish which, we are told in the Scripture, was taken by the young Tobias, at the command of the angel Raphael, was useful for giving sight to the blind, for healing disease, and for putting to flight the evil spirit; and, in point of fact, the narrative goes on to tell us that, by means of it, sight was given to the father of the young man, and the evil spirit that persecuted Sara, the wife of young Tobias, was put to flight. Optatus Milevitanus makes here a parallel between the fish and Christ, applying to both the words, illuminat; sanat; et fugat diabolum—as did the fish, so does Christ give sight to the blind; heal disease, and put to flight the devil. Here, then, we have a banquet at which the mystic fish is partaken of, that is, Christ. That it is the Eucharistic banquet is further evident from the baskets of bread; and the fish and the bread also allude to the multiplication of the loaves and fishes described in the sixth chapter of St. John, as we have seen, and which serve as the introductory miracle to the doctrine of the Blessed Eucharist. This is not a mere allusion to this miracle, much as such allusion imports. For this symbol of the fish too clearly refers to the Eucharist and to Christ Himself. In other places in these Catacombs we find a fish upon a trident, which is the cross concealed; and a fish alive, swimming, having on his back a panier of bread, and in the middle of the panier a bottle of red wine. There is, then, no doubt as to what we have before us: the seven Christians or disciples are partaking of the Eucharistic banquet, in which Christ is really present. It is He whom they are eating, to use the words of Christ Himself. When we take into consideration, dear brethren, the tradition of the Church, it is not possible for us to mistake the interpretation of this remarkable picture. But this is not all. I mentioned two lateral pictures. One of these presents us with a tripod, the well-known type of sacrifice in pagan art, which the Christians took because it contained in its idea nothing that was specifically pagan. Upon this tripod a sacrifice is offering by a priest whose hands are stretched out over the oblations, which are the same objects as are partaken of in the banquet—the fish and the loaf of bread. We have here the Blessed Eucharist, both as a sacrament and a sacrifice; and, lest there should be any doubt as to the nature of that sacrifice, the second lateral illustrative picture speaks an unmistakable language, for it presents us with the figures of Abraham and Isaac; of the ram, and of faggots of wood. It is well known that Isaac was the type of Christ in His Crucifixion; for, as Isaac took the wood upon his shoulders upon which he was to be sacrificed, so Christ took the wood upon His shoulders—the cross—upon which He was to die a sacrifice for our sins. This picture tells us, more clearly than words, that the sacrifice on the tripod is Christ's upon the cross, mystically represented in the Blessed Eucharist. We have, therefore, the Blessed Eucharist here before us, in the symbolism of the early part of the third century, both as a sacrament and as the Sacrifice of the New Law. Christian symbolism thus

comes to the aid both of Scripture and of tradition, perfecting, as it were, the proof of the truth
of the Catholic doctrine, which the authoritative
decisions of the Church have taught.   Of these
decisions, there are two I wish especially to lay
before you.   The supreme teaching authority of
God's Church is the ultimate judge of controversy, from the very nature of the case.   The first of
these dogmatic declarations is found in the Confession of the Fathers at the Council of Ephesus.
"We confess," they say, "that we approach to
the mystic benedictions, and are made holy, inasmuch as we are participators of the Flesh and
Blood of Christ."   The word used here, "benedictions," means precisely the Eucharistic offerings.   The second is the decree of the Council
of Trent, treating professedly of this doctrine
against the errors of the innovators in general of
the sixteenth century.   The words, therefore, of
this great council, legitimately called together in
the Holy Ghost, and speaking in His name and
by His assistance, must carry with them a weight
exceeding that of all argument or human authority.   In the fourth chapter of the thirteenth session we read : "Since Christ, our Redeemer, said
that what He offered under the appearance of
bread is truly His Body, therefore has it always

been the persuasion (or belief) in the Church of
God, and this now anew this Holy Synod doth
declare, that, by the consecration of the bread
and wine, a change is made of the whole substance of the bread into the substance of the
Body of Christ our Lord, and of the whole substance of the wine into the substance of His
Blood, which change has conveniently and properly been called, by the Holy Catholic Church,
transubstantiation."

Such, dear brethren, is the doctrine of the
Church of God concerning this wonderful Sacrament of the Body and Blood of the Lord. How it
discloses to us the secrets of His love for us! He
loved His own who were in this world, and He
loved them to the end; and in the midst of the
oppressive dread that was upon Him, on the eve
of His Passion and Death, unheeding our offences, He instituted this banquet. And what
a banquet it is! The banquet of the King of
Kings, where He Himself is the food of those
He invites; a banquet where He shows so much
desire of enjoying the presence and company of
His guests that He does not let them leave Him;
but, just as the material food of the body becomes one with them, He gives Himself to be
eaten by them that they may live by Him. "He

that eateth me, the same shall live by me." Nay,
more, if we approach worthily, as St. Augustine
says, we become what we have received: " Si
bene accepistis, vos estis quod accepistis." *
How is it possible, dear brethren, that, with
the evidence of so much love on the part of
our divine Saviour, there should be so many
who abstain from receiving the sacrament, or
receive it seldom, or approach it in a cold and
formal manner? Yet so it is. Jesus Christ felt
this so deeply that He menaces with death those
who do not come to the Eucharistic table : " Unless you eat the flesh of the Son of Man, and
drink His blood, you shall not have life in you."
And He bids the messengers go forth and gather
in the guests, by force if need be—"compelle
intrare." It is not creditable to our faith or to
our gratitude, dear brethren, if such a course
must be pursued with regard to us. Let us
quicken our faith in this great sacrament. It is
in a special manner the sacrament of faith. And
as Jesus Christ Himself said that to accept His
doctrine can only come from His Father, let us,
feeling how weak our faith is, and how deficient
is our gratitude, beg of Him to increase our faith,
and inflame our hearts with love for Him. Let

* Sermon 227.

us assist Him in so doing by frequent acts of love and adoration; by frequent visits to Him as He sits on His sacramental throne, or dwells in the quiet of the Tabernacle, speaking to us a silent and eloquent language we cannot misunderstand. At those moments heart speaks to heart, and we learn the vanity of earthly things; we enjoy the anticipated happiness of paradise; we understand the inestimable value of resignation to divine Providence, and of the perfect accomplishment of God's will. He becomes our Teacher, telling us how we may lead spiritual lives—even the life of angels here on earth. He, there, is a pledge not only of perseverance here, but of a glorious eternity hereafter. May this Holy Sacrament be such to you, dear brethren, is the blessing I wish you all. Amen.

Lecture XI.

ALTHOUGH the nineteenth century is an epoch of novelty and of invention, there never has been a period in which interest in the history of remote ages was keener, or the results of archæological investigation more satisfactory. The whole world is divided into two classes of seemingly opposite ideas. One is peering into the future, believing in the progress of humanity, casting on the past doubt which will not stand the test of principles often arbitrarily assumed. The other is matter-of-fact, does not discard the amelioration of the human race, but, rejecting unsustained theories and unfounded scepticism, looks to the past for lessons of truth and of wisdom, believing that there have been wise men and truthful narrators of what once was. The spirit of the former class, though not without its beneficial features, has been the cause of immense evil in casting aside cherished memories and traditions, and with them the principles which gave them life. Dazzling often with the electric brilliancy of their success, they have oftener led men into darkness impenetrable, and entangled them hopelessly in the meshes of illogical or unsound thought. The latter class, in quiet, plodding, persevering efforts, attract little attention, till suddenly a result is obtained, solid in its nature, durable in its effects, and triumphant in its vindication of historic truth.

To this latter class belong generally those who are engaged in the serious study of antiquity, not led by theory, but eminently inductive in their method, gathering facts, collating them, and patiently awaiting the fruit they hope for. Not a square inch of stone bearing the marks of the hand of man escapes them; a cuneiform character, a hieroglyph, a Greek letter, or a Latin date, invests the cold marble with an interest which gives it life and makes it speak in faltering accents first, then in language not to be mistaken, when, in union with its other parts, it tells of the past in a way that cannot be gainsaid. It is by such patient, painstaking care that the discoveries of Layard, of George Smith at Nineveh, and of Schliemann at Troy and Mycenæ, have been brought about. The schools of

Niebuhr and of Arnold may be aptly taken as
representing those who write history from theo-
retical standpoints, and who, influenced by scepticism, have rejected as fable what they could
not compass.   The spirit, however, which has
actuated Layard, George Smith, and Schliemann
is fitly shown us in the following words of Mr.
William Dyer, author of the well-known article
on Roman antiquity in Smith's *Classical Dic-
tionary*, and subsequently of the interesting and
valuable works on the histories of the City of
Rome and of the Kings.   At page 62 of his
introduction to the *History of the City of
Rome*, he says: "There is little motive to
falsify the origin and dates of public buildings;
and, indeed, their falsification would be much
more difficult than that of events transmitted by
oral tradition, or even recorded in writing.   In
fact, we consider the remains of some of the
monuments of the regal and Republican periods
to be the best proofs of the fundamental truth of
early Roman history."   This is an eminently
sensible remark; and I shall take its meaning as
our guide in the treatment of the subject of this
lecture, Early Christianity.   The sources, therefore, to which we shall look for information
will be the monuments of Christian antiquity ex-

isting at the present time. These are found scattered over a very wide range of territory—a range co-extensive with the old Roman Empire. They are of varied character—architectural, commemorative, sepulchral, artistic, in painting and in sculpture. Necessarily, in a brief lecture it would be impossible to go over such a field, and it is imperative that I should confine myself to a part only of it, and even then in a summary way.

Of all parts of the Roman Empire none could certainly reward investigation better than the Eternal City itself, its capital, which became the centre of Christianity, and the dwelling-place of St. Peter and of his successors, the heads of the Church in their respective epochs. Thither came Christians from all parts of the known world, and their piety made them devote their means to advance the material prosperity of the Church in the erection of churches and sanctuaries, and sepulchral ornaments. No portion of the Roman Empire, for these reasons, is richer in monuments of Christian antiquity than Rome with its territory ; and to its study I invite your attention. Even here, however, as the objects deserving attention are so numerous, to study profitably, it will be necessary to restrict ourselves to the exploration of the principal mines whence the treasures of Christian archæology are taken, the Catacombs, in which the Christians of the first ages were laid to rest.

The practice of depositing the bodies of the dead in the ground the Christians took from the Jews. It was not wholly a Jewish custom, as may be seen by inspecting pagan tombs discovered not long since on the Latin road. But the favorite manner, used by the Romans, was that of cremation, a custom born of the sentiment of repugnance human pride has to what is so revolting in death. The Jew, who believed in the immortality of the soul, reverenced the tabernacle in which it had dwelt, and in which he believed it was again one day to live. "In my flesh shall I see my Redeemer" was for him a sacred thought of deep meaning, and a tenet of unshaken faith. He followed the example of Abraham and of the Patriarchs, and laid his dead to rest in tombs cut in the rock or excavated in the soil, leaving, in humble submission to God, the remains to resolve themselves into their former elements, as ordained by the Maker of man. To these reasons of the Jews the Christians added a still more weighty one, the fact of the Saviour of man having thus been laid to rest. Every Christian wished to have his body buried as that of his Master, with whom he expected one day to rise again.

Before the Christian religion was preached in Rome the Jews were there, and possessed places of burial which remain at this day. Rome, being the centre of the world at that day, was the starting-point whence radiated roads to every point of the compass. These were the Ostian Way, the Latin Way, the Flaminian Way, the Nomentan Way, and the great Appian Way, the main artery of communication with the vast East, running across the Campagna in a straight line to Brundisium, and so much frequented as to receive the appellation Regina Viarum, "Queen of Ways." By this road St. Paul came to Rome, striking the Via Appia on his way northward from Puteoli, or Pozzuoli. Owing to the fact of its being the principal way out of Rome, it was selected by preference as the one along which the great families of the city erected the sepulchral monuments destined to hold the ashes of their members. Nothing could be more gratifying to family pride than that all who left or entered the great metropolis of the world, should see the statues of those whose deeds had made the family famous, and recognize, in

the taste and profusion of rich ornament, the
culture and wealth of those to whom the monuments belonged. For miles outside the city, the
Appian was lined with these tombs. This display disposition and circumstances made the
Christians leave to the pagans. They were obliged, more by public opinion than by law, to
bury as privately as possible. The law of Rome
was very considerate with regard to burial, and,
in fact, would serve as a model for more than one
of the present ruling states of the world. Even
during persecution burial was protected by law.
The jurisconsult Marcian (*Digest.*, i. 8, 56) says :
" Any one makes a place sacred when he places
in his property a dead body." Paulus, another
authority, states (*Sentent.*, i. 21, 4) : " Whosoever
lays bare a body permanently buried, or put for
a time in any place, and exposes it to the light
of the sun, commits a crime against religion "
(De Rossi, *Bull. Archæol. Sacr.*, an. 1865, p. 89).
He also says that " the bodies of criminals are
to be given up to any persons seeking them for
burial " ; though sometimes, through odium of
crime, especially of treason, it was not done.
The Justinian Code (iii. 44, 11) contains a decree
of Diocletian and Maxentius, of the year 290,
in which they say : " We do not forbid the bu-

rial of those condemned for crime and subjected to a well-deserved punishment." This was the law. But public feeling often sets aside law; and the Christians, with commendable prudence, took this into account. They therefore, as a rule, sought to bury where they would be least likely to be observed. The situations they sought were the hills around Rome, generally at the sides of the great Roman ways, not far from the city. A radius of about seven miles will include the most distant of the Catacombs, by which name are known the Christian cemeteries. The reason why the Christians sought the hills was because, as they buried deep under ground and not on the surface, they feared the water of the rivers getting into the tombs in low ground. Moreover, they found strata of soft rock, known as *tufa*, which cuts easily with a pick, and which, as long as it is underground, and not subject to the action of the weather, remains for centuries unchanged ; this being in great part due to the equable temperature of the Catacombs, and especially to the absence of frost. Having selected a fitting place for their cemetery, which was generally on the farm of some Christian, they began by sinking a shaft, or by striking out from some sand-pit into which projected this soft *tufa*. A corridor was excavated, seven or eight feet high by three feet wide, the earth being carried up and scattered over the farm, or thrown into the old sand-pit. When the corridor was completed, they made burial-places in the sides of it, according to the size of the corpse, and about a foot and a half in depth and height, which were hermetically sealed with tiles or marble slabs, inscribed with the name of the occupant, with figures, facts, or dates. When these burial-places, known as *loculi*, or *loculus* in the singular, had taken up all available space, a further excavation was made ; and, leaving a passage-way, it was the rule to throw the earth excavated into old corridors, sometimes completely filling them to within a short distance of the top. This is why the Catacombs are now said to be excavated : this filling is taken out. It was providential that the Christians filled up these corridors, for by this means the most valuable remains of Christian antiquity have been kept to our day. After burial in the Catacombs ceased, they were from time to time devastated, first by the Goths in the fifth century, and in the eighth century by the Lombards under Astolphus, in the year 755. This latter devastation was the worst of all. Tombs were violated, inscriptions and monuments broken to pieces and strewn around, mingled with earth and sand; and this mass contributed also to fill up the corridors. From this fact we can appreciate the prudence which causes the earth now taken from the Catacombs to be carefully sifted, and every portion of marble discovered in it to be jealously preserved for future use in making up the monument it belongs to, when the other parts will come to light.

From the corridors at intervals open out small rooms or chapels, known as *cubicula*. A *cubiculum* is usually not more than ten feet square; not always that. It generally has an arched tomb, known as an *arcosolium*, in which the head of the family to which the chapel belonged was laid to rest, or some distinguished person or martyr was deposited. The remainder of the chapel is lined with *loculi* for the members of the family. The walls between them were plastered and frescoed.

For my purpose it is not necessary even to enumerate the various Catacombs, and useless to attempt to speak of more than one. For this reason I take the most celebrated, as well as the one richest in what we wish to study—the Catacombs of St. Calixtus.

Riding out on the Appian Way, passing the Baths of Caracalla, the tombs of the Scipios, the Columbaria of Cæsar and of Pompey, you see before you the straight line of the Appian stretching on to the Alban Hills, crowned by the ruins of the temple of Jupiter Latialis, upon which stands a convent of the Passionist Fathers. On the right and on the left at intervals stand shapeless masses of masonry. What are they, or were they? They are the nuclei of sepulchral structures, which, covered over with beautiful marbles, and ornamented by statuary and alto-relievo work, were the pride of the old Roman families, and enclosed the ashes of their ancestors. About three miles out to the right stands conspicuously one of these masses, having beside it two trees which enable you to recognize, from a great distance, the site of the Catacombs of St. Calixtus. In the first century this *area*, or burial-place, belonged to the gens Cæciliana, a pagan family. Later, some of the family becoming Christian, it was in the possession of the lady, from whom that portion of this Christian cemetery is known as the crypt of Lucina. Here Christian burial went on during the latter part of the first, and during the second century, until every portion was so full of tombs that

it was necessary to enlarge the cemetery. Pope
Zephyrinus ruled the Church of Rome from the
year A.D. 202, and Calixtus was the archdeacon.
To him the Pope entrusted the charge of carrying out the work which made this the principal
cemetery of Christian Rome. Not all the excavation here, however, was done during the life of
Calixtus, for it was carried on as needed. As he
began it, his name has been given to it. Others
worked there as he had done. There is an inscription now in the Catacombs of St. Calixtus,
which reads as follows: "By order of his Pope,
Marcellinus, this Deacon Severus made a double
cubiculum, with its one skylight and arched
tombs." This description accurately corresponds
with the architecture of the place. Pope Marcellinus ruled the Church about the year 290,
so that nearly a century elapsed before that portion was excavated. Work of that kind, however, ceased not many years after; for burial in
the Catacombs began to be discontinued in the
first half of the fourth century. It is necessary
to call your attention to this fact, on account of
the epoch to which the monuments belong—for
those I am going to speak of belong to the first
three centuries. An inscription of Pope St. Damasus, cut by his celebrated workman, Furius

Dionysius Filocalus, and placed in the Papal Crypt of St. Calixtus, has these words:

"HIC FATEOR DAMASUS MEA VOLUI CONDERE MEMBRA,
SED CINERES TIMUI SANCTOS VEXARE PIORUM."

After speaking of the martyrs, confessors, and virgins buried there, for whom he had such love and veneration, he declares that he dares not desecrate their ashes by having himself buried among them. Damasus was Pope in the year 370. If a Pope thought the place too sacred for him, we may easily understand that these Catacombs had ceased to be places of burial. The incursions of barbarians later not only made the Catacombs inadvisable as places of burial, but counselled the removal of bodies to Rome.

The cessation of burial in the Catacombs certainly gives us sure data with regard to what is found in them. But there are other indications which serve to fix still more clearly the epoch to which the monuments we wish to use belong. In the crypt of the Catacombs of St. Calixtus, the wall of which has the representation of the Good Shepherd surrounded by His sheep, some of which are drinking of water flowing from the rock, on careful examination I found that the plaster, which served to close a *loculus*, lapped over the painting. Now, this *loculus* had been made by cutting through the painting, because all the other portions of the walls of the crypt. had become filled with bodies. Consequently this was an old fresco when it was cut through. People don't cut through new paintings. Eut, as I said, burial in the Catacombs ceased, or began to cease, in the early part of the fourth century. This fresco was old then. Other indications show it to belong to the groups of the early part of the third century, while art was still, flourishing. In fact, the judgment which artists, irrespectively of religious persuasion, have pronounced with reference to these frescoes of St. Calixtus, allots them to the early part of the third century. Just as those who are engaged in Biblical research learn to distinguish, with great accuracy, the epoch of codices or Bible MSS. by the material on which they are written, the style of lettering, and other less indications ; so, too, artists determine with great sureness, and very close approximation, the period to which paintings belong. Who cannot tell a pre-Raphael from a Giulio Romano? Who is not able to distinguish a Byzantine head from a Roman face of the time of the Cæsars? Just so is it with regard to the paintings of the Catacombs. Some might wonder how they could last so long under ground, and be inclined to doubt of their genuineness. Let them go to the Golden House of Nero on the Esquiline, admire the delicate and graceful figures of the Cripto Portico; and, when they have given expression and full play to their feelings of admiration of the art of the first century, let them visit the Catacombs and doubt, if they can, of the possibility of frescoes lasting eighteen hundred years.

The age and the style of these paintings are not the only interesting features they possess. Perhaps that which most attracts is their symbolical character. For they do not represent the tenets of Christianity in an obvious way, but in a manner easily understood when once explained, but not easily divined by an unskilled person. The reason of this is that in the first ages so great was the danger of discovery, and so merciless the shafts of ridicule aimed at the Christians, that it was deemed necessary to conceal under symbolical forms the sacred teachings of the faith. The very sacredness of these truths, more even than anything else, counselled the carrying out of the apostolic admonition "not to cast pearls before swine." Hence arose the "disciplina arcani," the economy of secrecy, which veiled and protected the mysteries of religion. In virtue of this economy it was not lawful for those initiated in the doctrines of Christianity to speak of, or represent publicly, certain of its tenets and usages; for example, the mystery of the Blessed Trinity, of the Blessed Eucharist, the sufferings of our Saviour, even the sign of the cross. The existence of this discipline is not only evident from the careful study of the remains of early symbolism, but is clear from the express words of the Fathers of the first centuries. Thus Tertullian, in his book addressed to a wife (*Ad Uxorem*, lib. ii. c. v. ed. Venetiis, 1744), says to one who is married to a pagan: "How will you escape the observation of your husband when you make the sign of the cross upon yourself or the objects you use? How will he not know what you partake of in secret before any other food? And if he should know it to be bread, he will not believe it to be what it seems." Origen says (Hom. ix., in Leviticum, No. x.): "He knoweth who is initiated what is the Body and the Blood of the Word of God; let us not, therefore, delay treating of things clear to those who know, but which cannot be disclosed to those who do not know." Pope Julius I. upbraids the Eusebians for speaking too openly about the Blessed Eucharist. In his Hom. xi., on St. John, St. Augustine writes even more explicitly: "If you ask a catechumen, Do you believe in Christ? he answers, I believe; and he signs himself with the sign of the cross of Christ. . . . Let us ask him: Do you eat of the flesh of the Son of Man, and drink His blood? He does not know what you are saying, because Christ has not yet trusted Himself to him." A fact made known a few years ago justifies fully this precaution of secrecy. In excavating the palace of the Cæsars, at Rome, a large room was discovered which had served as a waiting-room for the pages of the emperors. On the walls were found etchings, and one of these represented a cross, and on it a figure crucified, having the head of an ass. At the foot of the cross stood a figure, with his hand raised to his forehead, according to the Eastern mode of adoration, and underneath was written in Greek: "Alexamenos worships God." The original is preserved in the Kircherian Museum in Rome, and was brought to the notice of English-speaking people by the late Cardinal Wiseman. This is sufficient to account for the hidden manner in which the cross is found in the Catacombs. At one time it is an anchor, at another two diameters of a circle crossing each other at right-angles; again it is what is known as a gamma cross ⅃, or a trident. The earliest representation of Christ on the cross I have seen is a fresco of the early part of the third century, it being a trident with a fish upon it, the fish being a symbol of Christ, as I shall presently explain.

Let us go down the stairway that leads into the Catacombs of St. Calixtus. A descent of thirty feet brings us to a corridor, and a turn to the right leads us to the entrance of a crypt which gives the name by which these Catacombs were known to antiquity, *ad sanctum Xystum.* This subterranean chapel is about fifteen feet long by eight feet wide, with a skylight. Here were buried St. Xystus and twelve other Pontiffs. The bodies were taken out and brought to Rome in consequence of the ravages of barbarians already referred to. The slabs which enclosed the remains were broken and thrown on the ground; among them, those of Popes Eutychian, Fabian, Lucius, and Anterus, which have been recovered from the débris and replaced in *loculi.* Here was the inscription of Pope Damasus I spoke of, in which, after commemorating the sufferings and triumphs of those laid to rest in the Catacombs, he declares himself "afraid to disturb the ashes of the just." The portions of this inscription recovered are let into a piece of peperino, or stone of the Alban Mount. To the name *ad sanctum Xystum* was coupled the further appellation, *ad sanctam Cæciliam;* for tradition told of the burial of St. Cæcilia at this place. When Pope Paschal I., who became Pope the year 817, set about bringing the bodies of the martyrs and Pontiffs to Rome, he sought for her body, but could not find it. He tells us in the *Liber Pontificalis* what happened to him. He says he was one morning at St. Peter's with his clergy, when St. Cæcilia appeared to him and reproached him for giving up the search for her body, saying he had been so near to her in the chapel in which he had been, this crypt of the Pontiffs, that he could have spoken to her, face to face. On coming to himself he told his clergy what had happened. They proceeded to St. Xystus and St. Cæcilia, and found the body on the other side of the wall of *tufa* which separates the crypt from that of St. Cæcilia. She was in a sarcophagus, richly clad in a robe of golden tissue, with ornaments of gold upon her person ; the delicate body lay on its side, her head, nearly severed by the lictor's axe from the neck, enveloped in a light veil and turned to one side, the face downward, while her arms lay naturally with the hands in front, one hand with one finger extended, the other with three—she thus professing her faith in one God in three Persons. The remains were reverently taken up and carried to her house in Rome, across the Tiber, which had been the scene of her martyrdom, which she had left to be used as a church, and deposited under the high altar. There they remained until Cardinal Sfondrati, in the year 1599, by permission of the Pope, while repairing this church, opened the tomb and recognized officially the authenticity of the relics. The urn was opened in the presence of the cardinal and many others, among whom were Bosio, the archæologist, and Maderno, the sculptor, who made the beautiful statue of St. Cæcilia, so much admired, which is now under the high altar of the church.

Let us leave this place, though so full of edifying and refreshing memories, to wend our way through the labyrinth of corridors. Through an opening in the side of the crypt we find ourselves in a corridor lined on one side and the other with empty *loculi.* They once had occupants; the marks are there to show that—a tile still in its place, or a crumbling bone. Look well into them, and see the nature of the rock ; how the mark of the pick, as fresh as if made yesterday, makes it evident that it yielded easily to the stroke. Cold and heat have had no effect on it. We are too far underground for that. We pass on. Here right before us is an open doorway. We enter and find ourselves in a small room perhaps ten feet square and seven in height. It is full of *loculi*. But the ceiling and the spaces between the burial places have been plastered and painted. Over your head you see a representation of the Good Shepherd, so often met with in the Catacombs. At your left on entering you see on the wall a fresco-painting. There is a man with a rod in his hand, and he is striking a rock from which water is flowing. The subject is evidently Scriptural. It recalls Moses striking the rock in the desert. But it is not Moses. The very opposition, so marked in the New Testament, to every Judaizing spirit, would of itself exclude the frequently recurring figure of Moses. The rod in the hand, typifying power, might lead one to think it might be the prophet like unto Moses, to be raised up—Christ Himself. But Christ is not the one who strikes, but the thing struck; for, as St. Paul says: "They all drank of the spiritual rock that followed them, and the rock was Christ." A matter-of-fact argument helps us out of the difficulty and tells us who this figure is. Discs of glass have been found in the Catacombs at the tombs, illuminated in gold and black, which were covered over with a second plate of glass and annealed in a furnace, so as to hermetically seal the edges and so protect the picture. Several have come to light representing this picture we see before us, and one of them is now in the Vatican Library. Over the head of the man striking the rock is read the name *Petrus*, Peter. Peter is the antitype of Moses; he is the leader of the New Dispensation. So speaks St. Ephrem of Syria in his sermon on the Transfiguration on the Mount. Moses, the œconome of the Father, he says, saw Peter, the procurator of the Son

Adjoining this painting we see a group. A man is seated on the bank of a stream; he is fishing, and has caught a fish, which he is drawing out of the water. There is a boy standing in the water, and a man by his side is pouring water on his head. We are reminded at once of the words of Christ to the Apostles, "Henceforth you will be taking men." Here is the apostolic fisherman. The fish is the Christian.

This symbol of the fish is most interesting, and plays a most important part in Christian symbolism. So much importance did the early Christians attach to it that they made small fish of bone or metal, and carried them about as we carry watch-charms. It was the symbol of a Christian. It has been said that the Erythræan sibyl first used the acrostic 'ΙΧΘΎΣ; but the verses attributed to that sibyl are regarded as spurious. The acrostic itself was in use, however, from the early ages: first, because the five letters of the word are the initial letters of the five words 'Ιησοῦς Χριστος Θεοῦ Ύιός Σωτήρ. 'ΙΧΘΎΣ, therefore, recalls at once Jesus Christ, Son of God, Saviour. Moreover, the fish lives in the water, and so does the Christian by baptism. This made Tertullian, in his book on baptism, say: *Nos omnes pisciculi secundum* Ichthun *nostrum Christum; in aqua nascimur, et non nisi in aqua permanendo salvi sumus—*"We are little fish, after the manner of our great fish, Christ; we are born in the water, and only by remaining in the water are we safe." Then, writing of Quintilla, who denied the efficacy of baptism, he adds wittily: "The cruel Quintilla knows well how to kill the fish by taking them out of the water." Optatus, of Milevitum, in Africa, in the fourth century, in his comment on the book of Tobias, says that the fish caught by young Tobias, at the instance of the angel, was a type of Christ; for it was useful to cure blindness, heal disease, and put to flight the evil spirit. This, he says, is what Christ does: *illuminat, sanat, et fugat diabolum.* The fish, therefore, in Christian archæology, represents Christ and the Christian. In this fresco we have the Apostle who secured a soul for Christ, the soul being represented by the fish caught. How that soul enters into life is shown by the other figures, a boy standing in the water, and a man by his side pouring water on his head. This is baptism; and, what is of further value, we have here child-baptism. We see the early Church did not wait till a child grew up to man's estate to determine and choose for himself. She recognized God's right to our service and obedience from the first breath we draw, and consecrated the child to Him ere vice could taint it, and passion, grown strong with age, hold sway in the heart.

On the plaster connected with this group, and separated only by a line of color, is a man with a bed on his back. Here is the healing of the paralytic man of the Gospel. You remember, my friends, when and why our Lord wrought this miracle. On seeing this man lying in his bed totally paralyzed, Christ said to him: "Have courage, son ; thy sins are forgiven thee." The Jews murmured and said: "How can this man forgive sin ? Only God can forgive sin." Knowing their thoughts, our Lord turned to them and said: "Why do you murmur in your hearts ? Which is easier to say, Thy sins are forgiven thee, or, Arise, take up thy bed, and walk ? But that you may know the Son of Man hath power to forgive sin," turning to the paralytic man, He said, "Arise, take up thy bed, and walk." The man arose, and took up his bed, and walked. This power of forgiving sins Christ gave to the Apostles and their successors when He said to them: "All power has been given me in heaven and on earth. As the Father hath sent me, I send you." The Christians recognized, therefore, when they raised their eyes to this picture, the truth of the belief in the forgiveness of sins. Not only were they taught by the monuments of the Catacombs to so believe, but an inscription by Pope Damasus, who, as I have said, ruled the Church in the fourth century, and which is found in the crypt of St. Eusebius, tells how, in the beginning of the third century, a fierce controversy raged in the Church of Rome about the forgiveness of certain sins of a most grave nature. Eusebius was then Pope; the leader of the severe and gloomy Montanists was Heraclius. This man taught that those who had fallen away from the faith during persecution could not be forgiven. The Pope defended the doctrine of the Church that all sins, short of resistance to the Holy Ghost, could be remitted. The consequence was discord, strife, and bloodshed. The Pope was driven into exile, and on the shores of Sicily "left this world and life."

Passing from this fresco of the paralytic man, we see on the wall facing the entrance the most important and interesting of all the monuments in this room. It represents to us a central group and two pendants or lateral paintings belonging to it. The central group has seven persons reclining at a table, and upon the table are two fish.* In front of the table are eight baskets of bread. We immediately recur in thought to the miracle in the desert of the multiplication of the loaves and fishes. Yet that miracle, as we read in the sixth chapter of the Gospel of St. John, was only the prelude or preface to the

---

* This subject has been spoken of in the lecture on the Blessed Eucharist. As this is the proper place for its archæological treatment, I hope I shall be excused for introducing it again.

promise of the Blessed Eucharist ; and, therefore, though we have here an allusion to that miracle, the importance which the Christians gave to the symbol of the fish makes us realize that there is something more meant here. In a double room in the first portion of these Catacombs, of which I spoke as the crypt of Lucina, there are seen, on either side of the wall of the inner room, two live fish swimming, each with a basket of bread on its back, and in the centre of each basket a bottle of red wine. This makes it evident that the Blessed Eucharist is intended to be represented. Our Lord from material food elevated the mind of those He spoke with to the thought of a supernatural food, and bade them "seek not the bread that perisheth, but that which endureth unto life everlasting, which the Son of Man will give you," which was His Flesh and Blood. So here this fish and bread, while referring to the miraculous multiplication of the loaves and fishes in the desert, recalls the doctrine of the Blessed Eucharist in a way not to be mistaken. That meaning is made still more evident by the two lateral pictures. The one on the left hand presents us two persons, one standing near a tripod, with his hands stretched over the tripod, upon which are a loaf of bread and a fish.

The tripod is a symbol of sacrifice. It was a pagan symbol, to be sure; but the Christians were not narrow, and when symbols used by pagans were not specifically pagan, but suggested ideas common also to a true system of religion, they did not scruple to use them. This can be seen in the very accessory ornaments of this room we are in. So here, wishing to represent a sacrifice, they took the tripod, offered on it a loaf of bread and a fish, put the priest there with his outstretched hand in the act of sacrifice, and alongside a figure praying, with the hands raised just as the priest raises his hands at Mass—the Orante, or praying figure of the Catacombs, which here represents the Church. We see here typified the sacrifice of the Mass. The Blessed Eucharist is both sacrament and sacrifice. The lateral picture on the right makes still more evident what the picture on the left means; for it gives us a man, a boy, a tree, a fagot or bundle of wood, and a ram. The man is Abraham, the boy is Isaac, the tree represents the landscape of the mount, the bundle of wood was brought up by Isaac, and the ram is what was sacrificed by Abraham instead of his son. Now, we know that Isaac was a type of Christ, for he carried up the hill the wood upon which he was to be offered up; and Christ did the same when He carried the cross. There is, therefore, a unity in this fresco; the lateral paintings illustrate and explain each other, and both are closely connected with the central group, giving us, in this way, the Blessed Eucharist as a sacrament and a sacrifice, that sacrifice being the sacrifice of Christ on the Cross, offered in an unbloody manner, in the Mass.

The symbol of the tripod was of such importance in the eyes of the early Christians that not only did they repeat it often, but in one of the principal crypts in the Catacombs of St. Calixtus, near the one we are studying, it is to be seen, no one standing by it, in the most conspicuous place, having upon it two loaves of bread and a fish. This fact proves how prominent a place in Christian symbolism the tripod, the type of sacrifice, held.

Before leaving this subject I call attention once more to the seven figures here reclining at the table. All except the one in the middle have their right hands raised. This, it is well known, is the attitude of adoration. The middle one has his right hand stretched out over the objects on the table, which is the position of one offering a sacrifice. Taken in connection with what I have just described, the positions are most significant, and represent to us the sacrifice of the New Law and its great Sacrament, in which Christ is adored and offered under the form or appearance of bread and wine. On the walls of this room, near the ceiling on either side, are to be seen the frescoes of Jonas thrown into the sea and swallowed by the sea-monster, and afterwards thrown up on the shore. This fact Christ alluded to as a type of His death, burial, and resurrection. St. Paul says: "If Christ has not risen, then is our faith vain." The Christian hunted to death, knowing what a cruel fate awaited him when discovered, strengthened himself by the sight of these pictures which told of the resurrection with Christ, one day, in glory.

I shall close this lecture, my dear friends, with a few words on a subject regarding which Catholics are so frequently attacked, but which is to them a source of such great consolation and happiness: the devotion to the Blessed Virgin Mary and the saints. It has been stated, by more than one of the writers who in non-Catholic circles are looked on as authorities, that there are no representations of the Mother of God in the Catacombs. This is a mistake. There are several pictures of her that I have seen. One well known is in the Catacombs of St. Agnes, representing the Mother of Christ with her Child. The monogram of Constantine, the ☧ shows, however, it belongs to the fourth century. There is in the Catacombs of St. Calixtus one much more ancient, having been painted in the early part of the third century. It represents the three wise kings bringing their gifts to the new-born Saviour, who is in the lap of His Mother. She is seated on a throne, and extends with majestic dignity her hand to receive the gifts they bring. The whole style of this fresco is excellent, and shows how the arts were flourishing when it was painted. This same subject recurs frequently also in sculpture. There is a sarcophagus at the Lateran Museum in Rome, of the fourth century, which is most remarkable and valuable on account of its symbolism. Among other groups it presents us with the Blessed Virgin and her Child receiving gifts from the Magi. By the side of the throne, upon which she is seated, stands the figure representing the Holy Ghost, as can be seen by comparing it with the Holy Ghost in the Trinity figured just above it. He has His hand upon the throne, just as He is represented as having there. Besides these representations, we have those of the

saints, of those particularly who shed their blood
for the faith, by whose tombs are found the
small vials of their blood, gathered and preserved by the piety of the faithful as a sign of
their victory over persecution. Often on their
tombs, or by the side of the place where these
sacred remains reposed, was to be found the
prayer of the Christian, rudely painted on the
wall, and invoking the aid of the saint. What
especially strikes one, and in its spirit of beautiful charity touches the heart, is the expression
often found of prayer for the dead. The words
refrigerare, "refresh," is the favorite word for
signifying this prayer. It is, in fact, the liturgical
word of prayer for the dead. In the Canon of
the Mass the priest every day prays that God
may give to the departed *locum refrigerii*—"a
place of refreshment." In the Catacombs of
Prætextatus the Commendatore de Rossi, to
whom I am indebted for most of the information and explanation I have given you, found
the following words on a sepulchre uncovered
in 1851: *Deus Christus omnipotens refrigeret
spiritum tuum*—"May Christ the Almighty
God refresh thy spirit." In the same cemetery
of Prætextatus he found also this expression:
Refrigeri [*sic*], *Januarius, Agatopus, Felicis-*

sim. Martyres—"Refresh, O Januarius, Agapitus, Felicissimus, martyrs, the soul, etc." The inscriptions in the Catacombs are very frequently ungrammatical, a sign that they were written by rude people in the simple language of faith and feeling. In fact, it is a canon of archæology, the ruder and simpler, the more ancient; the more elaborate and polished, the more modern. In the Catacombs of Hippolitus, in the sixteenth century, Bosio found the words: *Refrigeri tibi domnus Ippolitus*—"May our master, Ippolitus, give thee refreshment." The word *domnus* is a title of distinction signifying "preeminence," as lord or master. In a tablet at the Museum of St. John Lateran, taken from the Catacombs or crypts of Rome, I have read the words: *Refrigera Deus anima*— the stone ending here, probably cutting off the final *m*— "Refresh, O Lord, the soul."

You thus see, my dear friends, how the tenets of the Christian faith we hold are illustrated by the discoveries of the Catacombs—how they show us the existence of a belief in the early Church in the primacy and hegemony of Peter, the Sacrament of Baptism, the forgiveness of sins, the Blessed Eucharist, the Holy Sacrifice of the Mass, the Resurrection of Christ, the veneration of the Holy Mother of God and of the saints, supplication for the departed. We look around us, and we find no church holding all these doctrines but the Holy Catholic Church of Rome. We recognize ourselves as one with the early Christians; were they to rise from their tombs they would come to us. Let us thank God for the perpetuity of His faith and for our possession of it; let us hold fast to it, appreciate it all the more feelingly, as we realize its miraculous life and its unsurpassed beauty.

APPENDIX.

MIRACLES AND MODERN SCEPTICISM—AN AUTHENTI-CATED CASE.

(Journal of the Fair, New York, 1878.)

In the spring of 1878 I was returning from Italy to America, and, leaving my route of travel, I went into Belgium. The reason of this going out of my way was because, some time before, I had read of an occurrence so remarkable that I wanted to look the matter up for myself. I had read, in fact, that a man had broken his leg; that the injury was what the physicians called a compound fracture; that he had been thus disabled eight years, the wound constantly discharging; that he had been visited by several medical men, who had pronounced the cure impossible; the only thing to do was to cut the leg off, as union of the broken parts could not even be hoped for. Just the same opinion would be given by our own surgeons here. Yet, all of a sudden, this man, who woke up in the morning in the pitiable condition just described, is seen walking about as sound of limb as any of the busy walkers one meets on Broadway of a morning. This, certainly, was extraordinary, and I was determined to look into the statement. I was well repaid for my trouble, apart from the charming scenery and interesting sights offered by the busiest little country in the world. I went at once to Jabbeke, a station on the railway from Ostende to Bruges,

where dwelt Pierre de Rudder, the man who was said to
have been cured, reaching this place on the first of
June.   I called immediately on the venerable curé,
the Abbé Slock.   He received me with genuine Bel-
gian hospitality.   When told the object of my visit,
he promised to do all he could.   Just then, he said,
De Rudder was out of the village, but he would send
word to him, and to any others I wanted, to come at
the hour I should name.

I named seven o'clock that evening, and besides re-
quested that some of those who, I had heard, had
assisted De Rudder in his sad state might also come.   In
the meantime, in company with the vicaire, I went to
see the only one of the medical attendants of De Rudder
we *found there*, Dr. Van Troostenberghe.   The doctor
received us very politely, and expressed his willingness
to answer any questions we might put to him.   We
found he had not seen De Rudder for two years, as his
physician.   He said the case was well known.   Two
years before he had seen the wound in the leg ; it was a
compound fracture and discharged a great deal ; he
thought some portions of bone had been lost, but he had
not seen these portions.   In fact, as I afterward ascertained from De Rudder, there was no bone lost.   The
doctor told us that both bones of the leg were broken,
the fracture being at the junction of the upper and middle thirds of the tibia and fibula.   He added there was
no cure for such a state of things.   The only resource
was to amputate.   He concluded by saying : "Art could
not accomplish such a cure as had taken place in De
Rudder."

All this only rendered me more desirous of making a
thorough examination in the evening.   At seven o'clock

I went with the curé to his office.   We found there
the following persons :

Pierre de Rudder, Edward Van Hooren, Marie Wittor-
zaele, Jean Houtsaeyer, innkeeper at Jabbeke, besides
the vicaire, or assistant priest.

The first person I questioned was Edward Van Hooren, a Fleming.   The vicaire translated my questions
and the witness's answers.   De Rudder had lost all hope
in man, and had been making a novena, or nine days'
prayer, to the Blessed Virgin of Lourdes.   There is a
small grotto of Our Lady of Lourdes on the property of
the Marchioness de Courtebonne, at Oostakker, near
Ghent, much visited by the people of the country
around.

De Rudder, not being able to go to Lourdes in France,
both from poverty as well as from his condition, resolved
to make a pilgrimage to this grotto.

Edward Van Hooren testified that he had seen De
Rudder on the eve of his departure for Oostakker, the
6th of April, 1875.   De Rudder told him he was going
to Oostakker.   He saw him turn his foot so as to put
the heel in front—"the heel where the toes were."   He
had several times seen De Rudder turn the foot and lower
part of the broken leg at an angle to the upper part of
it.   The last time he saw this was at 7.30 o'clock on
the morning of the day before he was cured.   The leg
on that day was much swollen, being larger around than
his head.   He saw him leave the next day for Oostakker.
He saw him in the afternoon of the same day, the day
he was healed, well and walking about.   Here the curé
made the remark that he himself saw De Rudder walking
that day without crutches, and well; that he had previously seen the wound, and the extremities of the broken

bone separated about three centimetres, or about an inch. Upward of two hundred persons saw him walking.

Marie Witterzaele, the next witness, also a Fleming, declared that she saw De Rudder, the day preceding the cure, at her house, at eight o'clock in the morning. He complained of his condition and showed his leg, bending it from side to side. He told her he was going to Oostakker. She saw the wound dressed about fifty times, and several times saw the ends of the broken bone come out of the wound in the skin. Both bones were broken.

I then questioned Jean Houtsaeyer, innkeeper at Jabbeke, who speaks French fluently. He said he had seen Pierre de Rudder only once prior to his cure. It was about two weeks before this event; he asked De Rudder what was the matter with his leg; De Rudder took hold of his leg and turned it almost entirely round, so that the toes were behind: "*Il mettait les doigts du pied par derrière.*" He showed the wound and the extremities of the bone, about two centimetres apart. The wound was about four centimetres square. He pointed to the inkstand on the table, saying: "That could have gone in it." The leg was slightly swollen. De Rudder told him the leg was almost dead, not feeling to any extent the piercing of a needle. He saw De Rudder the day he was cured; saw him walking, and did not recognize him, as he was walking without crutches. He offered to sign his name to what he had said.

Pierre de Rudder was finally questioned by us. He described his cure. He went to Oostakker the 7th of April, 1875, to pray for restoration to health. On reaching the grotto he took his place on the front bench. His leg pained him a great deal. The bench was crowded, and he was jostled by some one. This caused him so much pain that he left his place and went to a back bench ; here he became absorbed in prayer, and while in this state left his place and went to the statue of the Blessed Virgin.　When he came to himself he wondered how he got there, and looked around for his crutches ; he hadn't them by him.　They were at the bench.　He rose up, and found that he could stand perfectly.　The bandages fell, and would have slipped down to his feet had he not caught them.　The leg had resumed its natural size ; he was entirely cured.　He walked to the house of the marchioness and left his crutches there. In reply to my question whether he had lost any portion of bone, De Rudder stated that he did not remember.　His leg, for some days after the cure, was as if it were asleep.　In appearance it was like the other. He also stated that the wound used to swarm with worms ; and that, on the day he went to Oostakker, he had to put on it a large cataplasm of oak-bark to kill them. This assertion was confirmed by those present.　He showed me his leg and the scar that remains.　There is no inequality from callous or loss of substance of the skin.　He is sound of limb.　He can walk without the slightest difficulty or limping, there being no difference in the length of his limbs, nor any deformity in them.

It results, from this examination of the fellow-townsmen of Pierre de Rudder and of himself, that he was instantaneously cured of a compound fracture of the leg, complicated with a suppurating wound of dangerous character and swarming with worms ; that the cure was effected without defect in the broken limb ; that this also is the consequence of no material or medical treatment ; but that, having been given up by his physicians,

De Rudder had recourse to prayer, and that while praying he was entirely and immediately healed. We find no parallel for this case except in the miracles of our Lord, or of those the Church honors as her saints.

I cannot flatter myself every one is going to accept this fact as a miracle, or believe it supernatural, or will be induced by it to acknowledge the efficacy of devotion to the Blessed Virgin, or, finally, to enter the fold of the Church. Faith is a gift of God, and the Spirit breatheth wheresoever He will. Our Lord tells us, in the parable of Lazarus, in reply to the request of Dives, that some one should be allowed to leave the place of torments in which he was, in order to warn his brethren, lest they too should come to share his suffering : "They have Moses and the prophets ; if they do not believe them, neither will they believe if one rise from the dead." A fact like this will do good to those God wills should have the great gift of faith ; strengthen those who already possess it, and make them set a greater value on it.